I0691380

THIRTEEN TALES OF TEXTUAL AROUSAL

(VOLUME 2)

First Edition

Published by The Nazca Plains Corporation
Las Vegas, Nevada
2012

ISBN: 978-1-61098-297-9
Ebook ISBN: 978-1-61098-298-6

Published by

The Nazca Plains Corporation ®
4640 Paradise Rd, Suite 141
Las Vegas NV 89109-8000

PUBLISHER'S NOTE
Thirteen Tales of Textual Arousal: Volume 2 is a work of fiction created wholly by *Robin Anderson'* imagination. All characters are fictional and any resemblance to any persons living or deceased is purely by accident. No portion of this book reflects any real person or events.

Cover, Blake Stephens
Art Director, Blake Stephens

DEDICATION

For ANDREW (PRIAPUS) WICKS

"To Ream the Impossible Ream!"

THIRTEEN TALES OF TEXTUAL AROUSAL

(VOLUME 2)

First Edition

Robin Anderson

CONTENTS

CONTENTS CONTINUED...

SCHLONG OF INDIA

The film that changed Yamin Gunja's life was not the tiresome *Slumdog Millionaire*, an observation which would see the young man positively shaking with fury – 'I'd already made several millions by 2008, thank you very much!' – but *Chocolat*, made eight years earlier and telling the enchanting story of a young woman who opens a small chocolate shop in a repressed French village. The added factor that the 'shit and curry slop opera' was Indian (as indeed was Yamin) made the conclusion and comparison even more irritating. 'I didn't have to win a fucking lottery,' Yamin would expound, 'I worked my fucking butt off,' which – in more ways than one – he had.

Yamin's parents, like thousands more, having fled from Uganda, East Africa in the nineteen seventies to escape the reign of terror imposed by Idi Amin, arrived in England (or 'Benefit Britain' as it was later to become for thousands of immigrants from all over the freeloading world), where the industrious Mr. Gunja senior soon found his skills as an accountant (he had owned his own successful accountancy business in Kampala before The Great Escape) coming to the fore and had soon found employment with a small City establishment, Synde, Synde and Symons, whose reputation was more notorious than noteworthy. And although Mr. Gunja was soon drawing a reasonable salary (his skills at 'doctoring the books' soon becoming very apparent) he and his family were never to enjoy again the status and many luxuries of their former lives.

'You must become an accountant like Daddy!' was the daily mantra as preached by Yamin's mother, the comely Rita. 'See how successful he is? We now have a nice semi-detached in Ealing and own a two-tone Ford Fiesta! What more could anyone wish for?'

More, much more, young Yamin would think, looking disdainfully at the plump woman, complacently smug in her cheap nylon sari. However, the one thing Yamin could not have wanted more of was any additional length to his cock!

'My goodness! Talk about a baby cobra!' his father had exclaimed on first seeing the naked baby. 'Our son has a *lund* – no, a veritable *snake* – not only prestigious but truly gigantic! There will be much issue from this son!'

Like all good Muslims, Yamin's *cobra* soon lost its hood making his *lund* more like a dome than a decorative spire.

'It is indeed a penis of extraordinary length and breadth!' a proud Mr. Gunja senior would repeatedly inform his colleagues – or those pretending to listen – all of whom couldn't have cared less as to whether Yamin's penis was either prestigious, perfectly formed or downright pathetic.

At school Yamin's bulging shorts were always a great cause of derision amongst his contemporaries, *Gunja Gargantuan* being the nickname he'd had to bear for most of his young years. However, from being so embarrassingly cursed, the young boy (he had just turned fifteen) was soon to find his curse becoming a blessing.

'Gunja, I need to speak to you after class,' Mr. Hollingwood, the small, runty, bespectacled maths master had announced. 'Your marks are appalling and I suggest we seriously discuss some private tuition here.' The net result of such a comment immediately made young Yamin aware that Rita Gunja's ambitions for her son to become an accountant 'like Daddy,' would not be coming to fruition after all. What confused Yamin even further was despite Mr. Hollingwood's depressing declamation, his marks in class had always seemed higher than average. Unbeknown to young Yamin he had, in fact, indeed inherited Daddy's sharp mathematical brain.

Having previously enjoyed numerous mutual masturbatory sessions with Felix his elder (and envious) brother, Yamin remained unfazed when a trembling, sweating Mr. Hollingwood – 'You can call me Hugh in private!' – had placed his pale claw-like hand on Yamin's bony chocolate-coloured knee.

Contrary to Mr. Hollingwood's claim, Yamin – his brain immediately on red alert and whatever financial genes he'd inherited from his father going into overdrive – had quickly responded by taking the trembling hand and placing it firmly on his cobra, already stirring and ready to strike. 'Feel free, Hugh,' said the budding young entrepreneur, 'but contrary to what you say it'll cost you an A and not my usual B!'

Yamin was later to find that thanks to his extra tuition he soon graduated to an A plus.

Armed with the acknowledgement that a big cock was not a hindrance but an asset and his own massive chocolate-coloured cock could earn him extra brownie points (a double entendre he completely overlooked), along with Mr. Hollingwood's confidential 'spilling the beans' to Stephen Kember, the very fey art teacher, it wasn't long before Yamin – whose paintings represented a Rorschach test on Speed – was also getting an A plus for his 'mystical, magical interpretations!'

'My goodness gracious! Our son is going to do us proud!' chanted an ecstatic Rita to an equally ecstatic Mr. Gunja senior. 'We are indeed blessed!'

Unlike Hugh, Stephen wasn't satisfied with merely masturbating a naked, smiling Yamin or else making a futile attempt to swallow most of Yamin's chocolate cannon, Stephen Kember wanted to be fucked.

'Oh, I don't know about *that,*' muttered Yamin, the thought of how many A plusses *could* one be awarded quickly crossing his calculator-like mind.

'A present?' suggested the desperate Mr. Kember.

'Not a good idea,' said Yamin dismissively, 'How could I explain an expensive watch like a Rolex to my parents?'

'Expensive watch? A *Rolex*? I was thinking more along the lines of a Tee shirt from Primark!'

'I must then leave you,' said Yamin, pulling up his pants, the semi awake cobra/python teasingly disappearing back into his snowy white underpants so lovingly washed and ironed by Rita. 'Besides, Mummy buys all my clothes and she has never, ever set foot in a Primark. She only shops in Tesco or Harrods!'

'Oh dear,' said Stephen as the cobra, now back in the pristine underpants, lay snugly like a smug, coiled hose pipe. 'Oh dear, dear, dear!'

'Fifty pounds!' said Yamin.

'*Fifty*?' said the startled man.

'Yes, fifty pounds and I'll fuck you! But heed my terms please, Stephen (like Hugh, Christian names in private were de rigueur). It's fifty pounds per fuck, not per session. If I fuck you twice this afternoon, it's then one hundred pounds!'

'Let me see what I've got,' squeaked the fey, wispy man, taking his naked, scrawny frame over to his desk. Rustling through some papers in one of the drawers, he looked up beseechingly, 'I only seem to have twenty!'

'If I come back tomorrow and you have fifty, then I'll fuck you,' said Yamin grandly. With that he donned the rest of his school uniform and left. Later, Stephen Kember, consoling himself with a semi-flaccid wank, decided then and there to raid his holiday funds. After all, what was fifty, even a hundred pounds compared to the thought of accommodating Yamin's monster?

'I've never ever seen anything remotely comparable to his cock, even on the gay Super Paradise nude beach on Mykonos!' he muttered to the dismal drops of opalescent cum trembling on the aforesaid twenty pound note. 'Maybe I'll even stay at home this year,' he pondered, giving his pale, worm-like appendage a final squeeze.

The following afternoon a triumphant Stephen produced two crisp fifty pound notes resulting him not only being well and truly buggered twice with Yamin pounding away with the ferocity of a giant power drill but, as a gesture of good will, also having a balled fist thrust well and truly up into his well lubricated hole. Having been bent over his favourite leather chair, Stephen found Yamin's initial painful entry not so much a case of 'biting the bullet' but taking an enormous bite out the chair's worn leather arm.

Not only had Stephen Kember been fucked raw (dark red skid marks to his underpants would later verify this), the fact that his 'submission to the snake' as he had billed it, took place early in the evening and just before supper (the school catered for both day pupils and boarders), saw the teacher with little time to spare before joining other members of staff and the scholars in the dining hall.

Despite a quick shit in order to get rid of Yamin's copious spurts of hot cum deposited well and truly deep inside him, an unfortunate incident was destined to happen. As the housemaster's ponderous voice proclaimed 'For what we are about to receive,' Stephen, despite a superhuman effort of scrunching up his arsehole was unable to prevent the loudest, sloppiest, longest drawn out wet, squelchy fart vibrating loudly throughout the silent hall almost drowning out 'make us truly thankful.' Attempting to keep a straight face the bemused housemaster solemnly helped himself to the soup standing in the large tureen in front of him while the sudden clamour of banging cutlery, raised schoolboy voices and the general hubbub did little to hide Stephen's humiliation. Supper over, he made his way as discreetly as he could back to his rooms, his underpants sticking uncomfortably to his skinny shanks. Neither did Hugh's snide aside, 'I swear, because I was sitting down wind, I got a distinct whiff of curry carried along on that tsunami of yours, Stephen. Please correct me if I'm wrong?' offer any form of consolation.

'Fuck off,' Stephen had hissed, before squelching his way down the corridor. For several days mysterious farting sounds were made by innocent looking groups of boys as Stephen walked by, consoling himself that whatever the consequences, it had been the best hundred pounds he'd ever spent!

As word of Yamin's priapic penis along with his piston-like prowess spread along with his ready availability, so did the size of his fee. Now it was a hundred pounds per fuck! Mention of 'yummy Yamin' by Stephen to one of his non-scholastic friends, James Leach, a wealthy property developer (he had met Stephen at the aforesaid beach on Mykonos) saw Yamin's fee rising to an extortionate two hundred and fifty pounds per pounding!

Handing him a wad of notes – 'There's five hundred there and an extra hundred as it's your birthday (Yamin had just turned sixteen) and lots more from where it *came* from!' – James suggested the randy teenager meet up with a friend of his, Raymond Ramon, an ebullient 'celebrity chef,' easily recognizable from his popular afternoon television cook show, *Ramon's Recipes.*

Looking on as his mother proudly dished up one of Raymond's recipes – Rita was an avid viewer and ardent fan – Yamin would inwardly giggle at the thought of his parents reaction had he suddenly announced, 'Goodness Mummy! That Ramon's recipe for chicken done in coconut, cinnamon and lychees was very good indeed! Almost as good as the fuck Raymond and I had this very afternoon!' (He was inclined to become more Indian in his parents' company).

'You must see *Chocolat,'* panted Raymond from where he was perched on his plump hands and even plumper knees as a bucking Yamin thrust, pumped and pounded into Raymond's own squelchy, receptive, personal 'receptive *recipe'* as he coyly called it. Raymond also enjoyed talking volubly during sex unless his mouth was otherwise occupied. 'In fact,' squeaked Raymond between Yamin's increasingly vigorous thrusting and his own quickening gasps, 'I'll get it out on DVD and perhaps we can watch this over the weekend?'

'I charge an extra two hundred and fifty to sit watching a DVD while you wank me off,' said Yasmin not breaking his rhythm.

'Shall we say Sunday then?' gasped Raymond before starting to squeak, 'Ooh! Ooh! Ooooooh! I'm cooking! Cooking! *Cooking*!'

Yamin, his handsome brown face aglow, sitting alongside the satiated Raymond whilst idly playing with Raymond's cock (an achievement seeing Raymond, even erect, could only boast a plump three inches) looked at the tubby, naked little chef for a moment before saying, 'Two things Raymond; firstly, why do you work for that dreadful man? OK. It's his name on the door but you are the main draw and attraction.'

'He pays me good money.'

'OK, he pays you good money but *all* that hard earned should be going into *your* pocket.'

Raymond remained silent, his plump little cock becoming even more mushroom-like. He shifted uncomfortably, not attempting to meet Yamin's curious eyes (big, brown and beautiful).

'How much money do you actually *have,* little Raymond?'

'Why?'

'Because secondly,' said Yamin without hesitation while giving Raymond's receptive *recipe* a tender, little squeeze, 'I finish school next year, I have some savings and, if you are willing, let *us* open a restaurant together! Daddy I know would be most happy to give us his blessing and I am sure, with his contacts, able to raise suitable backing.' Yamin gave a laugh. 'Mummy would soil her sari at the thought of her Yamin being in business with the famous Raymond Ramon. So, what do you say?'

'Fuck me while I think about it!' said Raymond.

'That'll still be two fifty,' said Yamin beginning to prepare his own dish of the day for Raymond who had already placed himself in a sacrificial position over the arm of the sofa, 'plus a further two fifty for such a brilliant business suggestion!'

Rayyam opened the following year. With Raymond an established household name along with his flock of devoted fans, the restaurant, offering 'a pot-pourri of tastes sublime!' was an instantaneous success. But while Raymond may have been the wizard behind the scenes as he sweated away in the modern kitchen, it was the handsome, smiling young Yamin in his casual open-neck shirts from Gucci and his oh so carefully loosely draped linen trousers that saw the set of rich, salivating queens come flocking.

Salivating over the food was one thing but it was the salivating over the size of Yamin's carefully draped cobra which caused the most excitement. Bets as to the size of the *Gunja Gargantuan* – a name used tongue-in-cheek in one gay magazine's restaurant review and which was to stick – varied from a modest ten inches to a formidable fifteen. Raymond kept mum, Stephen kept mum, Yamin kept smiling and the diners kept coming.

Within three years two more *Rayyam* restaurants had appeared on the London scene. Raymond, now a mere shadow of his former ebullient self had seemed to have literally faded away behind a veil of steam and delicious cooking aromas.

A combined television appearance with Raymond and Yamin working in one of the state-of-the-art kitchens – Raymond labouring away and Yamin posing, his proud cock appearing above the worktop surfaces hogging the camera more than Raymond's busy hands – saw the reviews ecstatic about Yamin but barely mentioning his partner.

Rita, a regular at all the restaurants, found herself no longer looking after Daddy in Ealing but socializing more and more with her celebrity son. Yamin, an inveterate social climber, enjoyed nothing more than name dropping. 'Oh, I had dinner with the Duchess of York last night,' which, in reality meant, 'like all those other social climbing Z list idiots I paid a whacking five hundred pounds for a ticket to be sitting in the same room as her!'

One tongue-in-cheek tabloid – having wickedly described the plump, appallingly dressed woman as 'Riotous Rita!' – resulted in a technicoloured array of new silk saris which would have made even the most outrageous drag queen in a Gay Pride march look mediocre.

As Yamin's fame grew so, it seemed, did the size of his cock (by hearsay, if by nothing else). The clientele, gay and straight, grew more and more curious about the final, truthful dimension of the *Gunja Gargantuan.* No-one, or so it seemed, had been blessed with a viewing of, or better still, *possessed* by the tantalizing tube hanging so nonchalantly down the side of those oh so loose, floppy light weight trousers! Yamin, it must be noted, had eschewed wearing underwear deeming it 'bad for business.'

'I swear it's a *least* seventeen!' one frail, swooning young man claimed following an 'accidental' brushing by the aforesaid length as Yamin, making his continual rounds, strolled amongst the tables sweet talking the diners but paying particular attention to the purses containing the pink pounds.

Rupert, the young man claiming to have been personally nudged by the glorious Yamin ('How can a young man be allowed to be so beautiful,' sighed many an elderly gay, eyes misting over memories of a glorious misspent youth with another equally misspent youth!) would later remark to David (Dolores) Maddox, his best friend, 'when he touched me I just *knew* it was my destiny to be *his*!'

Rupert (nickname Regina due to his queenly bearing) set his trap with the innate skill of a lioness stalking an antelope, only this time the antelope in question being London's most blessed and most unobtainable!

Despite his blond, choirboy looks, Rupert's sexual encounters had been surprisingly few. However, remembering his cubs' motto of 'Be Prepared' (he never made the boy scouts) and having been witness to the *Gunja Gargantuan* Rupert determinedly set about doing just that. The biggest cock he'd experienced to date belonged to Dirk – the quirk – Donald, a fellow employee in the interior design showroom where Rupert worked and the rampant Dirk (the quirk referring to a strange bend in his length making it more boomerang than arrow) having caused Rupert to squawk and shriek on the first attempted penetration. 'It's so *big*!' Rupert had gasped on the first viewing of Dirk's rampant rod, 'And it's *bent*! I'll never be able to cope with that!'

'Oh, but you will,' reassured Dirk, liberally coating his erection with a handful of margarine taken from the office kitchenette (they were in the pattern room at the time) 'I'll be gentle, I promise!' Dirk's idea of being gentle had led to a shriek that, as Rupert later confided to an agog Dolores, even set the hanging pattern books 'all a tremble!'

Phase one of 'being prepared' saw Rupert making a discreet visit to his local Clone Zone, a well-known gay sex shop set in Soho's gay alley, Old Compton Street, where he purchased two butt plugs – one small, the other much, much larger – plus a dildo in the form of an enormous pink latex cock and balls cast from – or so the box claimed – the erect cock of a nondescript porn star going by the boastful name of Abel Semen. Coping with the first butt plus was fairly easy but Abel Semen proved to be an impossible agony and was put aside for a later attempt. Determined to be wholly accommodating on 'the night,' Rupert had carefully inserted the large butt plug which, apart from a discreet, lady-like bowel movement – Rupert would never have confessed to taking something as basic as a shit – remained in situ for a further two days. After finally accommodating Abel (they were now on first name terms) Rupert further astonished himself by being *able* to fully insert *up his arse* a large marrow purchase from the Food Hall in Harrods. 'After all,' as he had later quipped to himself as he stood, peering over his shoulder into a mirror and viewing the end of the marrow peering snugly from out of his fully stretched arse, 'if anything is going up my arse, I want nothing but the best!' Fully prepared, Rupert excitedly confessed to Dolores that he was now almost ready to 'set his trap.'

Phase two saw Rupert arriving at the main *Rayyam* for dinner a few Saturdays later. Making sure he reached the restaurant a few minutes ahead of Dolores and several other friends, Rupert spotted his chance. Yamin, wearing a purple shirt (Armani) along with a pair of loose, pale yellow linen trousers now made by his own tailor and cut so as to both flatter and emphasize the *Gunja Gargantuan,* was standing idly alongside the long bar chatting to a pale, wan Raymond who, having a respite before the evening rush, was slumped against the bar, a sparkling mineral water in front of him.

'Mr. Yamin?' Rupert, putting on his most winsome smile, looked up at the spectacular Indian.

'Yes?' said Yamin, flashing a pair of perfect dentally enhanced teeth.

'Rupert, Rupert Clarke: that's Clarke with an E!' Rupert said, giving out what he considered his best coquettish giggle. 'I just wanted to thank you, in person, for all the fun times and, of course, fabulous meals my friends and I have enjoyed in your delightful restaurant!'

'Why, *thank you* Mr. Clarke, or may I call you Rupert?' said Yamin, making a quick assessment of the young man's apparel. Shirt? OK, maybe Jaeger, the black and ivory silk stripe looks familiar. Nice pants, nice pert bum but too petit for the *Gunja Gargantuan*! Why, I'd probably split him in two, if not go right through him!

'Oh, Rupert, please!' He looked up at Yamin, giving what he described to Dolores as his 'come hither' look. 'May I, as a small token of appreciation, offer you a drink even though it *is* your own restaurant! I just happen to *know* you're a champagne man!'

'It's sparkling apple juice in a champagne flute, actually, and I never drink while working in my restaurants, but I wouldn't say no to a drink with you, *Rupert*!'

Rupert glanced nervously at Raymond who looked as if he could be eavesdropping on their little conversation. It was generally accepted that perhaps Raymond and Yamin were 'an item' though, glancing at the emaciated, exhausted-looking man, Rupert couldn't understand why. 'How on *earth* does a god like that ever want to fuck a tired old kitchen queen like Raymond Ramon?' he had often said to Dolores and their friends.

Plucking up courage, Rupert made his next move. 'Do you ever dine in other restaurants?' he asked.

'Of course,' smiled Yamin, thinking, trying to get me into being seen out with you in public, are you? Sorry, young Rupert, that'll never do! Yamin Gunja remains an enigma but I must say I wouldn't mind trying to fuck you! Instead, the smiling owner replied, 'But I also like an evening *in* now and then! So why not have supper with me one evening at my flat in Cadogan Square?'

Rupert's jaw literally dropped. 'Are you serious?' he managed to squeak.

'One hundred per cent,' laughed Yamin looking directly into the pair of widened blue eyes and thinking, Well, it has been ages since I fucked someone and, as I was thinking earlier, why not you, you're obviously gagging for it! 'How about tomorrow?' he added taking up a card from the counter. Reaching for an instantly proffered pen from the barman Yamin quickly wrote down the address. 'That's very private,' he warned the trembling young man, 'so don't lose it and under no circumstances is it to ever be handed out to anyone else! I've also written my mobile number in case you're unable to make it.'

'Oh, I'll make it alright,' breathed Rupert.

'Good,' said Yamin, his eyes giving a momentary flicker down towards his own groin. Following his glance Rupert couldn't contain a whispered, 'Oh my!' as he noticed the stirring of what appeared to be a mini fire hydrant slowly making itself known against the yellow linen trousers.

'As you can see you're already being welcomed!' murmured Yamin. 'However, Rupert,' – here the elegant man sat himself on a bar stool, turning his bulging trouser leg in against the bar – 'I am strictly a one night stand man. I never give a repeat performance. All you will be getting is supper and a one-off experience. That is my strict rule and I have never once and never ever will veer from it.'

'You mean…?' Rupert's mind was now in a whirl, 'You mean, all you want to do is fuck me and that's *it*?'

'What else did you expect, Mr. Clarke? You approached me, I've invited you to my home, you'll get supper as well as get fucked and then that is definitely *it*! End of story!'

'But I *love* you!' cried Rupert.

'Whoa!' said Yamin, standing up (his erection having rapidly dwindled at the turn of events), his face filling with alarm. 'Young man, I don't even *know* you! Look, forget dinner, forget I even suggested it!' He held out his hand, 'My card please.' Rupert sulkily took the card out of his trouser pocket but not before quickly glancing at the number again. 'And now, if you'll excuse me, my customers are starting to arrive.'

A look of concern on his handsome face Yamin hurriedly moved away from the strange young man, thinking, Christ, the last thing I need is a fucking demented stalker in my life!

A chastened Rupert managed, on leaving, a few whispered words with the extremely offhand owner. 'I can only apologize and ask you to forgive me for my gross earlier indiscretion, Mr. Gunja.' Taking a deep breath he quickly added, 'And if you would still like me to visit tomorrow and for tomorrow only, I'd be only too happy to do so.'

Ignoring the warning bells in his head, Yamin looked at the glorious blond young man standing so imploringly in front of him.

'Alright,' said Yamin, somewhat reluctantly, 'but only for tomorrow, for one night only. You do understand that *is* the rule?'

'One night only,' said Rupert, 'I swear.'

Taking Rupert aside, Yamin whispered, 'Very few men have been take to accept my cock,' he warned.

'I know,' said Rupert.

All day Sunday saw Rupert stretching his arsehole time and time again with Harrods best.

'One night stand,' he muttered, sitting fully impaled on the giant marrow wedged tightly between the foam cushions of the sofa. 'I'm going to trap you Mr. Gunja and, once in my trap I am never, ever going to share you with anyone else. I am simply never ever going to let you go!'

A smiling Yamin led the tense young man into the sumptuous flat.

'This is fantastic!' gasped Rupert, gazing awestruck at the opulent interior, his breath apparently taken away. 'Absolutely fabulous, like the owner!' he added in a strained, hoarse voice. Continuing to look around the elaborate room Rupert kept swallowing nervously, his hands visibly shaking.

'Drink?' said Yamin ignoring the last implication but alarmed by the young man's extraordinary nervousness. Christ, kid, he thought, relax, it's a fuck, not a funeral! 'A drink may help you relax,' he added lamely.

'I'd like a glass of wine, if that's possible,' stammered Rupert.

'Very possible, Rupert,' said Yamin with what he hoped was a disarming smile. 'I do happen to own three restaurants!'

'Of course, silly me,' said Rupert looking even more strained and decidedly uncomfortable.

'Look,' said Yamin, determined to get the young man to relax, consoling himself it was either nerves or else he would simply ask Rupert to leave. Besides, it was still early and he could always make an impromptu visit to one of the restaurants which was always good for the staffs' morale. 'Look,' he said again, 'Would it help you to relax if we went to bed right away, have a fabulous fuck and then have some supper, maybe even watch a film? I've an assortment of new DVDs, none of which I've had a chance to look at as yet.' He gave another smile, 'Supper can wait. I cheated, its only pasta which I mix with a sauce brought from the restaurant.' He gave Rupert a curious stare, 'Are you alright?' he asked, 'you suddenly don't look at all well.'

'I'm fine,' said Rupert with a strange, tiny smile.

'Here,' taking him by the hand Yamin slowly led Rupert through to a large, curtained bedroom dominated by a heavily draped four poster bed. 'Relax, Rupert,' he said, adding, 'Look, for some reason you seem very nervous. Whatever happens, I will never hurt you and if I am too big, I'll stop.' Yamin gave another soft laugh, 'After all, there are other ways we can make each other come. So, let's get this over with, have supper, watch a film and, if you're up to it, spend the night together where we can fuck and fuck again!'

Rupert gave another nervous swallow, 'Why did you say you were afraid I'd try to trap you?'

'Because I'm a free spirit, Rupert, and no one can or will ever *trap* me! I'm a man alone and always will be.'

'But I love you,' Rupert whimpered.

'Please don't go there, Rupert,' said Yamin warningly, his temper starting to rise but, along with his temper, a growing and terrifying excitement in which he found himself developing a wild desire to humiliate and even destroy the effeminate young man, so frail, so fuckable and also strangely frightening. 'Why don't I help you take your clothes off,' he said softly, rather like a mother speaking to a child. Rupert gave a small, submissive nod as Yamin began to undress him.

Standing naked together Rupert eyed Yamin's massive, engorged cock with a rapt expression verging on an almost religious fervour.

'It's all yours for the next few hours,' smiled Yamin liberally lubricating the *Gunja Gargantuan* with a hefty handful of hand cream taken from a large jar conveniently placed on one of the bedside cabinets.

Bending the slight figure over the edge of the high mattress Yamin roughly forced Rupert's legs widely apart, his own engorged bulbous head poised a few inches from Rupert's glistening hole which Rupert had insisted on lubricating himself.

'Try and *trap* me, Rupert? *Never*!' snarled Yamin beginning his entry into the young man's surprisingly loose arse. '*Trap* Yamin Gunja? No one ever will!'

'But I will! I will,' cried Rupert, his tearful, ecstatic face pressed into the downy bedcover, 'Just you wait and see! I love you Yamin Gunja and I will never share you, never let you go!'

'*Never*!' cried Yamin, his anger growing at the young man's incessant declaration of love and possession. Holding himself high above the supine, pale receptive body, he gave a mighty plunge, his giant cock disappearing deeply into Rupert's hot, moist cavernous hole. '*Never*!' he started to shout once more before his voice ended in a shriek of pure agony followed by another of blood curdling terror.

'My God! My God!' screamed the bucking, jerking Yamin, trying desperately to withdraw himself from Rupert's arse which, due to the screaming man's movements was being shaken about like a demented dog worrying a bone. 'What have you done?' screamed Yamin. 'What have you *done*?'

'Trapped you!' shrieked a laughing, crying Rupert, writhing and bucking in hedonistic ecstasy under the screaming man. '*Trapped you*!'

Yamin's shrieks and screams interspersed with cries of 'What have you done to me?' rang out unabated until, with an almost subhuman effort the sobbing Indian, sweat pouring down his handsome agonized face and from every pore in his twisting, turning body, finally managed to pull himself out of Rupert's gaping, blood-gushing arsehole. Looking down at his agonizing cock Yamin gave a wild cry and passed out.

'I told you I'd trap you!' said a laughing Rupert looking down at the unconscious man. Kneeling down he carefully moved the heavy mousetrap from the end of Yamin's virtually severed cock.

'Never be trapped? I bloody well trapped you, Mr. Gunja, didn't I?' Rising to his feet and looking down at the prostrate figure, and the legendary *Gunja Gargantuan,* now slain forever, Rupert gave a mirthless laugh. 'You should have allowed me to love you, Yamin, not have to trap you.'

He gently laid Yamin's mobile next to the man's outstretched hand. 'It could have been marvelous and such an easy thing to do. I'm going now, my true, true love and you will soon be in good hands once you ring emergency when you eventually come round.'

Giving a final look filled with what could only be described as pure contempt, Rupert nodded at the viciously sprung trap, its' sharp metal bar completely embedded inside the head of Yamin's still bleeding cock. 'You said I looked tense? Well, who wouldn't, walking around having inserted a set mouse trap up one's arse?'

THE WOMAN WHO COUGHED ON A BUS

Miriam stood nervously by the bus stop, her thick, ungainly woolen coat pulled tightly around her squat, bulky figure, the coat slightly incongruous seeing it was a mild September morning and, though still quite early, the sun was making a brave attempt to make its way through the banking clouds. Before she could stop herself, Miriam – already shivering profusely – gave another cough, not a *cough* cough, but one which seemed more of a nervous cough than a cold cough.

Receiving a disdainful glance from a scowling middle-aged woman standing nearby, Miriam gave a weak smile of apology, quickly covering her mouth and nose with a tissue scrambled for from one of the coat's copious pockets.

'Some people,' muttered the woman before moving pointedly away from the pale, sniffling, dark-haired girl.

A spasm of shivers coursing through her now starting to heavily perspire frame, Miriam noted, with a mixed relief and dread, the familiar red bus trundling up the busy road towards the stop. Holding out a shaking hand she stood, eyes glazed, mumbling quietly to herself as she waited for the bus to come to a halt.

Stumbling, she managed to clamber onto the waiting vehicle, pressing her travel pass shakily against the panel by the driver's window before making her way down the narrow aisle. As expected at this hour the bus was full but one young man, a polite smile on his handsome face, on seeing someone so noticeably in distress and not at all well, stood up. 'Please? Would you like to sit down?' he enquired solicitously, obviously concerned by the nervous young woman's state.

'Oh, err thank you,' mumbled Miriam, another nervous spasm causing her to cough violently into her hand.

A faint grimace of disgust on his face, the young man pressed back against the sullen, blank-faced, packed-in passengers blocking the rest of the aisle.

Miriam, her hand to her face, sat down slowly onto the still warm vacated seat, her ample form pressing against the effete young man sitting next to her.

'God!' said the young man, giving an indignant shake and pressing closer to the window. 'Get a life,' he mumbled, 'or better still, go on a diet!' before going back to staring fiercely at the book he was reading.

Miriam coughed again.

'Oh, for God's sake!' muttered the young man, 'Some people!' followed by a hissed, 'Imported peasant!'

This time Miriam's cough came out as a raucous bark, followed by a series of body shaking hacking sounds.

'Excuse *me!*' snapped the young man, making a great show of standing up and putting the book back into a small holdall. 'Excuse *me!*'

Deliberately crushing the heavy-set girl's knees against the back of her seat, he squeezed himself past her and, joining his former travelling companion was heard to sibilantly say, '*Honestly,* Charles! Did you have to be so fucking chivalrous and give up your seat to such a pig? I've probably gone and got some ghastly form of flu – *swine flu* more than likely – as a result of that little showering of germs!'

'Jesus, James, not so loud!' hissed an embarrassed Charles.

'Not so loud?' retorted James querulously, only to have question obliterated by Miriam going into a further violent paroxysm of spluttering and hacking.

'I *told* you we should have taken the tube!' James continued, 'and, whether you like it or not I'm getting off this cattle truck at the next stop!'

Much to the annoyance of the other passengers and making a great show of pressing the bell with an even greater show of pushing his way through the congested bodies, James finally made his way off the bus, followed – he was smug to note – by a red-faced Charles.

'Thank *God* for some fresh air,' sniped James. 'Not only was that woman a filthy bitch, she positively *stank*! Talk about the unwashed masses!'

Glaring after the departing bus he and Charles were literally blown off their feet as the bus exploded.

TWISTED TAXI

'Some weekend to look forward to, huh?' said Rupert glaring around the small, damp sitting room of the cottage. 'If this is their idea of a cozy, country getaway, no wonder they always stay up in bloody town!'

'Cheer up!' smiled Bob, dumping his overnight bag on the uneven wooden floor, 'Once we get a fire going and a set up a few candles, why, it may even appear romantic!'

'Always the fucking optimist!' laughed Rupert. 'Come here, you great softie!' Taking a grinning Bob in his broad arms, he gave the young man a tender kiss. 'Sorry,' he whispered, letting go of his lover, 'but I really *did* think when John and Jan offered us a place, an "away from it all," they didn't mean a place away from *it all,* all being the basic creature comforts!'

'You spoke too soon!' called Bob from the doorway leading to the next room. 'There's a massive state of the art TV set in here along with a stash of DVDs plus what looks like a radiator. In fact,' – and here the voice became slightly muffled – 'I've just turned it on and it seems to be working! Check it out in the sitting room!'

'*Eureka*!' cried Rupert, 'There's also one in here. Give me a second and I'll get this turned on as well.'

'And then me!' came the camp reply followed by, 'The kitchen's not too bad either!'

'Perhaps I did speak too soon,' laughed Rupert walking into the low beamed room. 'Cozy,' he had to admit, 'but before we do any more exploring, how about opening a bottle of wine and then, if we've courage enough, climb those stairs to what could be either paradise or purgatory! What do you envisage?' he added, opening a cupboard and taking out two glasses while Bob, bottle in hand, began foraging inside several drawers for a corkscrew.

'*Voila!*' cried Bob, holding a corkscrew aloft, 'Our first success to the start of several other varied screws!' Giving a mock frown, he added, 'In the dank, dark shadows of upstairs I envisage a large four poster bed, drapes and all! How about you?'

'A not-too-comfortable divan, and not even a queen-size at that!'

'So, bring your glass, *mon brave*, and let's take a look!'

'Well, not quite a four poster but a very, very nice bed, if I may say so, Mr. Stevens!'

'You may indeed, *Mrs.* Stevens! Shall we, er... christen the bed now or would you prefer to do your Dora domestic act first and unpack prior to being suitably savaged?'

'Oh, Mr. Stevens! Surely by now you must realize I simply *adore* christenings. All that splashing around with your formidable font never fails to make me feel well and truly christened!'

'You know the rules! Off with those christening robes and let's get *fonting*!'

'So,' said Bob, smiling at Rupert from his lumpy, lopsided armchair, 'know anything about this village to whose arms we've committed ourselves for the next three days?'

'Not a lot. John said there's a very pleasant local pub called – would you believe? – *The Queen's Arms*!' laughed Rupert. 'In competition with the queen's appendages we also have a village shop- cum-post office, an estate agent, one or two other shops – no Gucci I'm afraid – plus an old church dating back to Norman times. The church – you no doubt will be riveted to know – still serves whatever devout followers it can lure from the local inhabitants of one hundred or so.' He gave another laugh. 'Only problem, if we're going to take our *Don't drink, Don't Drive* slogan seriously, it's a good two miles walk from here to there and back!'

'Wow, now an example of *your* other font! Where on earth did you get all that wild, riveting information?'

'From the lovely Jan, no doubt in anticipation that we'd quickly change from seeing is disbelieving – or grieving! – to "well, maybe it's not so bad after all!" She does say the pub serves a very good meal so, maybe dinner tomorrow?'

'And why not? Now, let me see how that quiche is doing and while you're opening another bottle, I'll toss the salad. Then a DVD or two? I brought several new ones from the local video shop, one of these being *A Single Man* which means we can masticate and salivate over Mr. Firth, all at the same time!'

'Idiot!'

'Yes, but an adorable one who has, according to a certain person sitting opposite, the world's only arsehole with a built-in Magi Mix!'

'Good morning, raunchy Rupie!'

'Good morning to you too, young Bob!' Rupert, smiling fondly at the young man curled up alongside him gave a long stretch which was inadvertently accompanied by a loud fart. 'Oops!' he grinned, 'Sorry, Bobs! *Not* intended!'

'Apology accepted!' laughed Bob moving over and snuggling against Rupert's hairy chest. 'Besides, your farts, like your font, are special.'

'Special?' Rupert grinned down at the young man, mussing his hair affectionately. 'How on *earth* can a fart – even one of mine – be special? A fart is a fart with the only difference being – as far as I can make out – one possibly more pungent than the other!'

'Ah, but that's where you're wrong! *Your* farts always seem to carry the slightest suggestion of aniseed!'

'Now you're bullshitting me!'

'Oh, and definitely that too!' added Bob with a yelp as Rupert gathered him together if bear-like hug.

'So, plans for today? It looks as if it's going to piss down.'

'So much for a country ramble then,' said Bob, his relief apparent. 'Maybe a drink in the *Queen's Arms* before lunch and then an afternoon of more DVDs with a bit of the old Magi Mix thrown in?'

'Why not? It'll give us a chance to suss out the place and if this bloody weather deigns to clear, we could even walk there and back, a trial run as if it were.'

'I don't I approve of the word run!'

'Quite,' laughed Rupert. Giving the smiling, blond young man a broad wink, he added, 'Perhaps, in your case, I should have said a trial *skip* or maybe even a *mince*!'

'Careful,' said Bob, his eyes twinkling, 'or else Mistress Mince here may simply shut up her hardware shop for the rest of the weekend which means *no* Magi Mix, *no* meat grinder and certainly no mincer, if you catch my drift!'

'Perish the thought of a *Closed* sign on the shop!' laughed Rupert, 'so let's make that march instead of mince, shall we?'

'*Much* more appropriate!'

'Good! But also remember, young Bob, even drum majorettes profess to march!'

'For *that* remark may I suggest you get your beautiful fart funnel out of this bed and fetch a bottle of that Pinot I put in the fridge last night! OK! OK! I know it's only eleven o'clock but we're here for a dirty – no, make that *filthy* – weekend so let's make it a pure bacchanal of drink, more drink and dirty desires!'

'How can one resist?'

Two bottles later the cheerful couple set off, hand in hand, along the muddy track leading from the cottage up to the main road. A watery sun, making a brave attempt to filter its way through the low, grey scudding clouds, helped add an air of gaiety to the scene, the old trees bordering the track sparkling with reflective droplets of water glistening on their leaves and branches.

'We'll hold hands until we reach the main road,' Rupert had announced on leaving the cottage. 'After all, we don't want to scare the locals!' Hand in hand the two jumped nimbly across the shining puddles, skirting the larger ones until they reached the turnoff to the cottage.

'Christ!' panted Rupert, 'I haven't had so much fun – or exercise! – since God knows when! And I'm dripping! Wearing our macs wasn't exactly the best idea for this impromptu hurdle event!'

'As I said on leaving, be prepared, Rupie!' laughed Bob, shrugging off his own mackintosh (both borrowed from the coat rack in the entrance hall to the cottage) and folding it over his arm. 'Bet you a blow job though it'll be raining again by the time we decide to walk back!'

'You're on, rain or no rain!' laughed Rupert. 'However, if it starts pissing down we'd best stay on in the pub for the rest of the afternoon and have an early supper.'

'No way, José!' laughed Bob, 'I've a new little number I'm planning to launch tonight which I'm quite sure *will* startle the locals!'

'You can be such a tart at times, Stephens!'

'Yes, but a tart with a heart who even approves when you fart so you can't really ask for more, or can you?'

'No, I suppose not but the mind is certainly going into overdrive!'

'Oh shit! No some kind of fart festival, I trust? Farts and more farts beneath the duvet!'

Rupert stopped in midstride, turning to give his companion a lewd grin. 'I was thinking more of fart *fodder*!'

'Jesus, Rupie! We've had this conversation before and you know my answer to that is to simply scat!'

'I take it you mean scat as in quickly run away?'

'I most certainly do!'

'Pity.' Rupert gave a rueful smile. 'I was hoping when you said earlier a bacchanal of drink, more drink and dirty desires you were possibly considering doing the *one* thing with me we've never done and only watched on DVD.'

'Sorry, Rupie, farts yes, but fart fodder? A definite no no!' Seeing an expression of genuine disappointment on his lover's face Bob adding consolingly, 'But let's not rule out a golden shower or two! You like those don't you, Rupie?'

'Yes, but let's face it Bob, we've done practically everything with each other and did vow to leave no stones unturned. Just once?'

'Let's play that one by ear, please Rupie! You know it's the one thing I somehow…' here Bob's voice trailed off into a whisper.

'I know, sweet thing! Forget about it!' Giving a chastened Bob a bright smile Rupert added, 'We're here! Now, butch up young Bob! You're about to experience – for the second time today – being in the arms of another old queen!'

The pub, a picturesque thatched white-washed and half-timbered timbered building stood facing a small green surrounded by the obligatory shops and several cottages.

'Postcard pretty,' admitted Rupert, draping his mac over his left arm while pausing in front of the low, sturdy oak door to the pub. 'We were wrong about the bed,' he hissed at a grinning Bob, 'so how do you envisage the locals?'

'Pure Hieronymous Bosch! All toothless, slightly gaga and with hayseeds in their hair!'

'Touché!' Pushing open the door Rupert gave Bob a gentle squeeze on his left buttock. 'Lead on, MacDuff!'

There was a distinct lull in the conversation as the two men entered the pub before making their way over to the bar counter from where a smiling, buxom blonde called out a cheery 'Good afternoon, gentlemen! You must be the guests staying up at the Bumble!'

'If you mean the cottage belonging to Jan and John Edwards, then you're correct,' smiled Rupert in return, 'but we didn't know it was called the Bumble!'

'Should be called the bloody Tumble,' came a raspy voice, followed by a deep, raucous cough. 'Surprised it's still standing!'

'Quiet, Tom Fellowes!' laughed the blonde, 'You *know* it's considered one of the prettiest cottages associated with the village and it's even said that Geoffrey Chaucer slept there!'

'Yea? No wonder the poor sod had to go on a pilgrimage!'

'Very funny Tom, maybe you should try one of them one day!' giggled the woman giving out a light laugh at her own humour. She turned her attention away from the surly man, his large figure hunched up alongside Rupert and Bob. 'Ignore him!' she laughed, 'I'm Belinda, by the way, proprietor of *The Queen's Arms* and the grumbler on your left is Tom, Tom Fellowes, our local gloom and doom merchant!' She nodded to a small group standing at the far end of the bar, 'And over there another three regulars, Mick, Dick and Simon, all farming lads.' Jutting her chin in the direction of the other drinkers, she added proudly, 'And over there some out-of-towners come to try out our restaurant. Our little restaurant has quite a reputation for its food.'

'So we've heard,' replied Rupert, giving another smile, 'and we're planning to try it later.'

'Oh, well I'm sure you'll find it up to your expectations,' smiled Belinda, 'Now, what can I get you gentlemen?'

'I'd like a gin and tonic please,' said Bob, acutely aware of four pairs of eyes regarding him with open hostility. Christ! he thought, maybe Rupie was right! Red cotton chinos, Gucci loafers and an open neck blue, orange and red striped shirt are not really country! He glanced over at Rupert who was now standing some distance away studying the lunch and dinner menus. And Jesus! We're wearing *exactly* the same clothes! Not intentional but simply a London Saturday habit!

Taking a sip of his drink – Where's the gin, Bob wondered – he glanced discreetly in the direction of the three burly figures now muttering among themselves. Hmm, thought Bob, not bad if you're in to belligerent, butch roughs, not bad at all! As if reading his thoughts, the tallest of the three, a bald, thickset man in his mid-thirties, his bare muscular arms heavily tattooed, suddenly glanced directly at Bob, meeting his look with one of pure loathing and utter contempt. Unable to prevent himself, Bob gave a sudden start, spilling his drink down his front.

'Fuck!' he cried before he could stop himself. Flushing a deep crimson he quickly added, 'Oh, forgive me Belinda, I didn't mean to swear, nor did I mean to spill my drink!'

'Not to worry, dearie,' smiled Belinda, handing him a dishcloth. 'Mop yourself up while I get you another.'

'Thanks,' grimaced Bob, dabbing at the front of his shirt, 'Oh, and Belinda,' he called across to the woman as she began to prepare his drink, 'less tonic please, in fact, could you make that a double?'

'Of course, dear,' said the smiling woman but not loud enough to cover a low, growled reply coming from the direction of the three farmhands. 'Not only using foul language in front of a lady but complaining about the drinks she serves as well.'

Bob looked hesitantly in their direction only to be met by three pairs of eyes staring defiantly at him. Shit! he thought, forget Hieronymous Bosch, these fucking three would make the Terminator think twice! He turned anxiously towards Rupert who appeared to be deep in conversation with a new arrival, a smart, middle-aged woman with the brightest red hair he had ever seen and whose companion, perched on the bar stool alongside her, appeared to be an enormously plump, snuffling Pekinese dog.

'Ah, Bob!' smiled Rupert. 'Finished with your ablutions, have you? Try more tonic next time!' He gave another laugh, 'Now come and meet Marjorie, she run's the village shop and local post office.

My *ablutions*? thought Bob, pity you didn't notice the pure and utter homophobic venom of those three troglodytes and testosterone Tom here! I certainly have!

Introductions over, Bob was soon in animated conversation with Marjorie ('call me Marge!') and Rupert who, along with Peter the Pekinese, were now seated at a table in a cozy corner to the room. The two men were soon to learn that Marjorie, before retiring to Haddinstone, the name of the village, had been a croupier in one of London's most prestigious casinos. 'Before old age and calories decided to become my greatest companions!' she had added with a laugh. 'It was Belinda here – we met back in London when she too was a croupier and we'd stayed in touch – who suggested I take over the village shop which was up for grabs! This I did, along with the post office franchise and here I've been for the past seven years, a true case of living happily ever after!'

To Rupert and Bob's delight they found Marjorie to be both fun and as the wine flowed – lunch having been forgotten – highly camp and a brilliant raconteur of outrageous stories concerning the rich and famous who had frequented the casino.

'We're planning on having dinner here this evening, Marge,' said Rupert, giving Bob a quick glance and receiving an affirmative wink in return, 'and, if you'd care to join us – Peter too, of course! – we'd be delighted.'

'Are you *sure*?' carolled Marjorie, 'Why, I'd love to! The food, by the way,' she added *sotto voce*, 'is very good indeed. Bert, Belinda's other half, is a cordon bleu chef and the little dining room through there' – she nodded in the direction of a small doorway – 'draws people from nearby Newmarket and as far away as Cambridge.'

'So I've heard,' smiled Rupert. 'In fact, Jan Edwards did say Bert's skills have even been written up in one of the London Sunday papers.'

'Yes, he was!' cried Marjorie excitedly, 'and also in one of the foodie magazines!' She gave the two a mischievous smile. 'And don't for a moment imagine I didn't know what you must have been thinking when you first arrived! You thought you were returning the Dark Ages here in Haddinstone, I know I certainly did!'

Having been advised by Marjorie to make a dinner reservation the three agreed to meet up again at eight o'clock. 'And don't worry about walking home later,' Marge added having been told the two had walked to the pub that afternoon and planned to do the same regarding dinner. 'There's always Will, our local taxi. He's teetotal and actually works days in Cambridge but his home's here. Will is only too obliging on nights, when necessary, to ferry some of Belinda's more merry guests back home!'

'Oh, I'm sure we'll be able to stagger back,' laughed Rupert.

'Well, just remember,' laughed Marjorie, 'and if you'll excuse the pun, where there's a Will, there's a way!'

'Who'd have thought a place like Haddinstone boasted such a glorious fabulous fag hag!' laughed Rupert as they walked back to the cottage in the late afternoon sunlight, the rain clouds having disappeared.

'Not only an outrageous fag hag but also four of the most terrifying homophobic louts one would ever wish *never* to meet,' said Bob, giving an exaggerated shudder and clutching Rupert's hand. 'Apart from that Tom character, didn't you notice those three gorillas standing at the other end of the bar?'

'No really, Bobs. But I wouldn't let them bother you. Local yokels and all that!' Rupert gave a loud chuckle, 'Come to think of it we did, and still do, look fairly outrageous in our getups! One should have remembered Haddinstone is *not* Chelsea!'

'Tell me about it,' said Bob, letting out a small snigger. 'Perhaps I'd better wear the proverbial sackcloth and ashes for dinner!'

'What, and spoil Marge and Peter's fun? Don't forget she *did* refer to you as doppelgänger to Oscar Wilde's Bosie!'

'That's what worries me! Not only one Marquess of Queensberry, but four of the fuckers!'

'That was delicious,' announced Marge, 'and thank you both! I must say, I haven't had so much fun for a long time. Promise Marge and Peter you'll be *bumbling* along to Bumble cottage more often! Oh, listen to me!' she added with a shriek, '*Bumbling* to *Bumble*? How much of that glorious wine *have* you had, Marjorie Mayhew?'

'So why not a glorious liquor to round off the evening?'

'Oh, Rupert! I thought you'd never ask! Why, I'd simply *adore* a Drambuie!'

'Your wish is my command,' laughed Rupert.

Drinks ordered the three, now once again seated back in their favourite corner of the pub, sat chatting amiably until Marjorie, stifling a yawn, announced it was bedtime for her and 'Peterkins.'

'Before you go Marge (Marge having refused an escort back to her cottage saying 'I'm just across the green.') can I ask you for Will's telephone number? I don't think Bob and I could really face that trek back in the dark, added to which I forgot to bring a torch!'

'No need for his number,' smiled Marjorie, 'he's sitting over there by the bar talking to Belinda.'

'I thought you said he was teetotal,' questioned Bob.

'Oh, but he is, dear! His tipple is simply a wild Coca Cola with a dash of lime juice! Come along, I'll introduce you on my way out.' Picking up her handbag and lifting a dozing Peter from the spare chair, she lead Rupert over to the slight figure sitting at the bar counter. 'Will!' she said, tapping him lightly on the shoulder, 'I'd like you to meet a friend, Mr. Bainbridge, who, you'll be pleased to hear, requires your services!'

'Hi, Will!' smiled Rupert, holding out his hand as the man slowly turned round to face him.

'Evening,' whispered Will, staring fixedly at Rupert with black, lack lustre eyes. 'How can I help you?'

Momentarily taken aback, Rupert, in retrospect, would say to Bob, 'My immediate reaction was Christ! The could-have-been model for Edvard Munch's *The Scream*! A skull-like head and face perched on the thinnest neck I'd ever seen and a frame matching the head, more skeletal than human! And being dressed entirely in black, black roll neck, black trousers with the only other colour being a pair of bright red trainers? Spooky! Real Spooky!'

'How can I help you?' asked Will again, giving a glimmer of a twisted smile and displaying a set of grey teeth.

'Oh!' said Rupert, shaking himself out of his reverie and looking wildly round for Marjorie, only to see her exiting through the main door. 'Err... a lift please, for my friend and myself, back to err... Bumble Cottage? In, let's say, ten minutes?'

'I'm ready when you're ready, Mr. Bainbridge,' came the sepulchral reply before Will turned his attention back to Belinda and his drink.

'Jesus, Bob! You may have been given a fright by your three weirdoes at lunchtime but, if you take a discreet look over at out about-to-be driver, think more Ghost Train than taxi!'

'A port in any storm, as they say!'

'Ah, Bobs! The eternal pessimist! And talking about port, why not another schooner before we hit the road with Doctor Death?'

'Right Will, we're ready.'

'Then follow me, gents,' came Will's whispered reply with an added, 'I like your jacket, sir,' his dark eyes looking appraisingly at Bob's lime green velvet blazer. 'Pretty blue trousers as well,' he added with a twisted, grey smile.

'Jesus, Rupe! I have never been so relieved to get inside a front door before – even if it isn't ours! That guy was the pits, and he stank!'

'Tell me about it! But, as you said, any port in a storm and it is now storming outside. Not only rain but just listen to that bloody wind!' Handing

Bob a glass of wine he gave him a long look before speaking. 'What would you say to us going back to London first thing?' He gestured to the small sitting room. 'This place, the pub, the locals – apart from Marge – gives me the creeps!'

'Rupie, not only are you the most glorious guy on the planet, but you're also a fucking mind reader!'

'Good, then that's settled. So, why don't you put on some music while I go and fetch another bottle, we've almost killed this one!'

'What was that?'

'What?' Rupert turned to look at Bob, snuggled comfortably in the crook of his left arm.

'I thought I heard a bang – or even a crash?'

'Probably a branch off a tree, there is a helluva gale blowing out there!'

'Hmm, yes, probably.' Bob gave a small yawn, 'So, back to London tomorrow which means, my big, bold, bawdy lover, we'll be able to trot along to Mark and Tim's barbecue after all.'

'Which you what you really wanted to do all along!' laughed Rupert softly, giving Bob a gentle nuzzle in his neck. 'If I believed in black magic, I wouldn't have put it past you to set this whole scenario up!'

'My dear Rupie,' giggled Bob, snuggling closer to his lover, 'I can assure you not even the highly imaginative Bob Stephens could have dreamt up those three hideous homophobes, that testosterone-infused Tom and certainly not weirdo Will!'

'No, you're right; even the other other Stephens – or Stephen – Stephen King, would have found them a challenge!'

'There,' said Rupert, a good half hour later, scrambling the last glowing embers with a poker, 'beddy-byes my friend.

Taking Bob by the hand he took the lead up the narrow stairway. Reaching the door to the main bedroom Rupert pulled open the door, stepping into the dark room, Bob, still holding his hand, close behind.

'Fuck!' muttered Rupert fumbling for the light switch. 'I'd forgotten. Bedside lamps only; wait here.' Making his way slowly across the room he reached the bed where, feeling for one of the lamps, he finally found it and switched it on.

'Christ!' he gasped on seeing Will lying fully clothed upon the bed, his red trainers gleaming like fiery beacons in the lamplight, any further reaction being quelled by blood curdling scream from Bob. Turning towards his friend Rupert saw four giant shadowy figures standing by the broken window. 'What the…' he began, only to be silenced by one of the figures hurling itself across the room and grasping him savagely by the throat. 'Shut it! Fag cunt!' grunted a deep, guttural voice as two more figures grabbed a shrieking, struggling, kicking and scratching Bob.

Four days later the charred remains of a BMW coupe was discovered by a lone hiker in a little-used wood several miles from the university town of Cambridge. Inside the burnt out wreck were two bodies, later identified as a Mr. Rupert Bainbridge and a Mr. Robert Stephens, a wealthy gay couple from London who had gone through a civil ceremony three years earlier.

It was later revealed the couple had been weekending in a small village a good half hour's drive from Cambridge. Mr. William Hoskins, a local taxi driver, had informed the police he'd driven the two – both very drunk – back from the local public house, *The Queen's Arms,* back to the cottage where they had been staying. A solemn Mr. Hoskins had also confided to the police how the two gentlemen had been in 'truculent and argumentative state, the one accusing the other of' – and here the modest man had almost been too embarrassed to utter the words – 'fucking around!'

Mr. Hoskins concluded his statement by confirming the last words he'd overheard from the couple had been, 'And if needs be, to show my love for you I'm even prepared to die for you!'

The expression on the witness's face had said it all.

'Bloody pervs,' he was to proclaim in the pub several weeks later after a verdict of suicide had been reached. Taking a sip of his drink he added, 'Filthy, soiled, disgusting buggers, all of them! They should all do what those two did and top themselves, leaving the world to the likes of us, decent, God-fearing, normal folk!'

'Quite right, Will,' muttered Mick, one of the three farmhands.

'Fucking right!' muttered Simon, another of the trio.

'Castrate the lot!' suggested Dick, 'not that they put their balls to any normal use!

'Make them eat them, though they'd probably enjoy that!' chortled Tom, his remark causing a quick, cautionary glance from Will.

'Nice jacket, Will,' smiled Belinda thinly. 'I'm sure I've seen one like that before somewhere,' her comment causing the four pairs of eyes to slowly home in on the startled taxi driver.

'You fucking idiot!' hissed Dick a few minutes later, Belinda having gone through to the storage area behind the bar, 'She'll obviously put two and two together and remember that's the jacket the bloody little queer was wearing when here for dinner that night.'

'I doubt it,' sniped back Will, his eyes narrowing, 'as far as I'm concerned I got it at a *Bring and Buy* sale in Cambridge. Try and see is anyone can dispute that? And who can even prove it belonged to the poof!' He gave a snigger, 'Proof, poof, geddit?'

'Very funny, Will,' growled Dick, 'but I wouldn't wear it in here again.' He turned to his two companions, 'let's go and Will, Tom, catch up with you later at the farm, OK?'

'See you there,' mumbled Tom with a similar reply from a disgruntled Will.

'Bitch is too dumb to put two and two together,' he muttered after the three had left. He sat staring morosely into his drink before giving Tom a sly glance. 'It felt bloody good, didn't it, Tom?' he said softly.

'Bloody good,' said Tom, giving a small, sinister smirk, 'and that's why we're going to do it again but finding a couple in Cambridge. Two of those poncey students for starters and that, my friend is where your expertise comes in so don't let those three get you down.' He gave a snigger, 'Dick probably wanted the jacket for himself but it wouldn't have fitted!'

'What we did,' continued Will, 'didn't make us queer and I'm looking forward to giving it another go!'

'Me, also,' muttered Tom, before giving one of his rare grins. 'But Christ, that big bastard certainly fought back, especially when Dick stuck his friend, stomach first onto that pitchfork!'

'And didn't the friend squeal like a stuck pig?' glancing towards the storeroom door he quickly hissed, 'She's back!' Taking another sip of his drink, Will continued, 'So I said to this guy, sorry guv, but no dogs allowed in the cab and you know what? As quick as a flash he produces a twenty quid note and said, "This plus the fare?" So what could I do?' He gave a raw chuckle, 'Still finding dog hairs on the carpeting but what are a few hairs when it comes to twenty quid?'

Will, having dropped off Rupert and Bob, had turned his cab around before making his way back to the main road where he sat waiting, as arranged, for Tom, Simon, Dick and Mick to join him. 'Fuckin' hell,' he muttered to himself as another gust of wind shook the cab, 'Anymore of this and we'll have to call the whole bloody thing off.' Lighting a cigarette he sat listening to the radio, his mind running over what the five had agreed earlier. The openly homophobic five men had never, until the few days before, ever witnessed such an obviously gay couple as Rupert and Bob in Haddinstone.

Apart from the occasional gay outsider, usually a couple or a group visiting *The Queen's Arm* solely for the purpose of dining, the bar itself have never attracted any gay clientele. Those who had come to 'experience the food' were merely subjected to a few glares and derogatory remarks among the small group of regulars.

Dick, with a penchant for beating up or harassing gays – 'queer bashing' as he called it – had been involved in several skirmishes in the bigger towns nearby and once had made a special journey to Brighton where he, along with an eager-to-please Simon, a curious Mick, and another group of 'queer bashers' had spent a vicious evening beating up unsuspecting members of the gay community celebrating the aftermath of a Gay Pride march. The fascination for such acts of violence had remained dormant until that fateful Saturday evening. Claiming he was feeling 'sick' and 'about to puke with disgust,' he had quickly cajoled Simon and Mick into 'doing something with those two filthy queers.' A few quick words with Tom had convinced Dick that an evening with 'a lesson to end all lessons!' was necessary. It was at Tom's suggestion, whose skills as a handyman had seen him doing the odd bit of work on Bumble cottage and thereby knowing the layout, they broke in via the upstairs bedroom window – there was a convenient ladder in the garden shed – while it was Simon, with his fascination for the macabre, who'd suggested Will 'lie in wait' on the bed. 'You look like fucking Dracula' had been his sniggered observation. 'Jesus, if *I* turned on the bloody light and saw you lying there, I'd shit myself!'

'Maybe you can do that later as well!' had come the laughing response, 'that's another thing those bastards like doing, shitting on each other!'

'But what it they don't want a taxi?' queried Will.

'Still nothing to stop us being there when they do get home,' had been the sharp reply.

Rupert's reaction to finding Will followed by Bob's hysterical outburst not only caused their five tormentors adrenalin to race but also saw Dick and Simon becoming immediately sexually aroused, Simon's enormous cock swelling grossly against the struggling, writhing Bob, Tom's massive hand muffling his screams. As Will struggled to hold Rupert he was joined by Mick while Dick helped Tom and Simon retrain a desperate Bob.

'Let's fuck him!' panted Simon, staring wide-eyed at an equally panting Dick, 'let's show him what real guy can do!'

'Not here!' panted Dick, 'Not here! Let's get them back to the farm, no evidence then!' Glaring at a wide-eyed, struggling Bob, he hissed, 'Shut the fuck up!' before knocking him senseless with a lethal right handed punch. Spinning to face a demented Rupert, struggling manfully in the grip of both Will and Tom, he repeated the action.

Bundling their two unconscious victims into the back of Simon's 4 x 4, Will, accompanied by Dick, followed in his taxi with Mike close behind, driving the couple's car. Minutes later the three vehicles came to a halt outside a large, dark storage barn filled with farming equipment and bales of hay.

'Right,' said Simon, eyeing an unconscious Bob and Rupert, 'let's start with the *real* frail fairy of the two.' He nodded towards Mike, 'Better tie up the big bugger before we waken him to watch the fun and get this one starkers and spread out on that bale of hay.' Unbuckling his belt he leered at Dick and the other three. 'OK, OK, so you haven't fucked a guy before but whose to know and besides,' here he gave Mick a lecherous wink, 'maybe you'll find it even preferable to the odd sheep which we all happen to know, Mick, you've enjoyed fucking in the past!'

'Never…' Mick began protesting but was silenced by Simon raising his big, beefy hand. 'Dick and me *saw* you mate, in Plover's Field, not once, but several times so don't give us any of your denying bullshit!'

'Right,' Simon said again, shucking down his jeans, his bulging erection pushing out against his grimy underpants. 'Get a load of this,' he added, unsheathing his cock which, freed from the restraining fabric, sprung up almost vertical, its thickness almost a match for the big man's wrist as he pulled back the grungy foreskin. Grabbing a handful of axle grease from a nearby can, Simon, his face contorted with excitement, began lasciviously lubricating his throbbing length as Tom and Will knelt a naked Bob over a bale of hay. 'Wake the other one!' he commanded Tom, pointing to a bucket of water nearby. Without hesitation Tom threw the contents over Rupert, now securely tied and having been propped against another bale.

'What the fuck…!' spluttered Rupert, his eyes bulging as he took in his grinning captors standing looking down at him in the dim light. 'What,' he began before a rough gag torn from a piece of sacking was forced into his mouth, a deep groan coming from the very depths inside of him as he saw Simon viciously impale his oil-smeared cock deeply inside his lover. Simon, having given a roar of animal-like triumph as he came inside Bob, was quickly followed by an equally well-endowed Dick. Using Simon's oozing cum as a lubricant he thrust himself into the still unconscious Bob.

A hesitant Tom, after the minimum of persuasion took his turn while a shuddering Will, unable to retrain himself, simply ejaculated over the head of the supine young man.

'He'll be too loose by now,' snorted Mick, 'and besides I don't really fancy the idea of you guys' cum on my dick, nor all that guys blood and shit! I'll do the big guy but still have some fun with the little one first.' Glancing round the shadowy barn his eyes lighted on a pitchfork leaning against another stack of bales. 'Maybe not as thick as you and Dick, Simon, but let's see how far I can get the handle of that pitchfork up the little faggot!'

Striding across the hay strewn floor he grabbed the pitchfork and, turning it upside down, rammed the handle deep into a groaning Bob now semi-conscious, his groans turning into a loud piercing shriek as the handle went in deeper and deeper.

Rupert, his eyes wild and his mouth bleeding from where he'd tried to bit through the gag and making a superhuman effort, somehow managed to stumble to his feet.

'Oh ho!' chortled Simon, his long thick cock semi-hard again. 'Lover boy's last stand, I believe! Sit down, faggot,' he cried, giving Rupert a brutal punch in the chest. Turning back to Mick he shouted, 'Enough Mick, enough of impaling him up the arse! Let's impale him properly from the front for lover boy to see!'

Deeper groans emanated from a sweating, desperate Rupert as he struggled to get to his feet again, his eyes widening in even further horror as Mick, helped by Simon and Dick, moved the screaming, struggling Bob over to where Will and Tom, bracing themselves, stood holding the pitchfork upright. Bodily lifting the frail, wriggling figure they brutally impaled him stomach downwards, the gleaming spikes bursting out from the young man's back. With a small sigh Bob slumped forward onto the pitchfork, a trickle of piss running down his still flailing legs followed by a soft phut as he shitted himself.

'Dirty little sod right up to the end!' sniggered Will. Turning to a grinning Simon he added, 'shall we give lover boy a final taste of his little friend?'

'Means we'll have to take his gag off!' cut in Mick.

'Wait!' cried Dick, 'what have we here?' Striding to a corner of the barn where a silent tractor stood, he picked up a petrol can and a funnel. 'Stop the shit with some straw,' he shouted, before returning with the funnel held aloft in his brawny arm, reminiscent of the Statue of Liberty. Nodding to Will and Tom he added, 'Bring shitty over to his friend and, when I give the word, hold him above the funnel and the pull the plug.' He gave a snort, 'A last supper with a difference!'

With Mick firmly holding down Rupert's head and Simon sitting on his bucking legs, Dick quickly tore of the gag and, before Rupert could utter one last, hoarse, despairing scream, jammed the funnel deep into the choking man's throat. 'Now,' he cried, 'Shit away.'

As Tom pulled out the plug of straw, shit, blood and leftover cum gurgled down into the bowl of the funnel and down into Rupert's throat. It took the five men all their strength to hold down the big man as he struggled desperately, choking on the deeply embedded funnel. After what seemed an eternity Rupert was finally still, his final humiliation being fucked by the five men before being dragged over and thrown alongside Bob.

'OK guys?' asked Simon, his eyes bright.

'Damn sure we're OK!' cried Mick, giving his crony a high five.

'And if you're thinking what I'm thinking, the answer is, yes, and why fucking not?' Giving out another loud laugh he proceeded to slap the others affectionately on their backs. 'And while we're about it… Mick, did you?'

'A case of lager? You're damn right I did.'

'Great, and once we've toasted the success of *Finish the Faggot,* let's get rid of the bastards and yes, Will,' he added with a laugh, 'that jacket looks great on you!'

Two days after Will's gaffe in the pub, Belinda drove into Cambridge for appointment with the Chief Inspector of Police regarding what she, as 'a morally bound citizen,' felt 'a crucial factor' in connection with a recent local incident.

TOSSING THE CABER

Sweet little Morag McClean's father, big, genial, red-haired Hamish McClean, threw back his large head and gave a roar of loud laughter. 'That's a good one, Rory!' he managed to gasp in his broad Scottish burr before giving another guffaw, 'Good, bloody good!'

Rory Cameron nodded discreetly in the direction of sweet little Morag, who, sitting on a nearby stool, her tiny thumb stuck in her rosebud-like mouth, was listening wide-eyed to the banter between her daddy and daddy's friend. 'Careful of your language in front of the wee lassie,' he admonished softly, his accent almost as strong as that of his still guffawing colleague. 'Such words are not right for such sweet, wee ears.'

'Aw, fuck that!' chided big Hamish. 'The wee girlie's heard worse from that worthless ma of hers and her stepfather. On that I'd bet you another wee dram of that fine Johnny Walker!'

'Women?' responded Rory with a shrug and a grin. 'Impossible to be with; impossible not to be with.'

'Aye, but at the moment I'm doing just fine with the wee Morag in my life, and bet or no bet, I wouldn't say no to another whisky!' He glanced across at the small, silent figure huddled on the stool in the darkened corner. 'You alright there, wee Morag?' he questioned, attempting to focus on the small form. Morag, her thumb still resolutely stuck in her mouth, nodded she was, her dark eyes staring at her father unblinkingly.

Just as Rory was about to rise and make his move towards the small bar, Hamish turned in the direction of the blonde, buxom barmaid who had been standing wiping the over-wiped glasses, a small smile playing on her rouged lips as she vaguely listened to both the men's banter along with the softly playing radio on a shelf behind her. 'Hey, Jenny girl!' Hamish beckoned to the plump, motherly figure. 'Rory's come up with a winner here! Did you happen to catch any of it in between listening to that dreary shit on your wee radio?'

'Language, Hamish McClean! Language!' Jenny, her smile broadening, nodded towards the silent little girl. 'Remember, please, there are ladies present!'

'My apologies, Jenny,' chortled Hamish, not at all apologetic. He glanced around the small, snug bar which, apart from the four of them, was now empty. 'Rory was about to buy another round so why not come over and join us until another customer comes in? Have a wee drink and let Rory retell his tale!' Hamish gave out a deep chuckle. 'It's a good one!'

With Jenny comfortably ensconced in a large, old wingback chair and facing the two grinning men opposite her, Rory prepared his new audience for the retelling of his story. 'It's a true telling,' Rory said earnestly to an already giggling Jenny – it was at this moment he glanced theatrically over his broad shoulder towards the closed main door – 'And it could even involve a certain gentleman known to us all; but the setting and the wee lassie? Well, the village and the setting I leave to your imagination and as for the wee lass, let's call the little lovely, Tessa.' He glanced across at Morag. 'But I must tell you, she was nowhere as pretty as our own wee Morag here!'

RORY'S WICKED TALE:

Well Jenny, there was this wee lassie – rather like our little Morag over there – on her way to visit her auntie in a small neighbouring village. Although warned by her mother <u>not</u> to take the short cut across the fields, our little heroine did just that, skipping along through the bright purple heather and singing happily to herself.

Suddenly she spotted big Ben McTavish working on installing some new fencing to the edge of his land. Ben, as always, was in a white singlet and kilt, his brawny arms glistening in the bright sunshine, his strong legs supported by a pair of sturdy boots. The little girl, knowing Ben as a friend of the family, quickly changed direction, skipping over towards the sweaty giant of a fellow.

'Mornin' wee Tessa,' smiled Ben.

'Mornin' Mr. McTavish,' the cherubic wee lass responded sweetly, looking up in awe as the massive man hefted another wooden post into its hole, the muscles in his arms rippling like huge serpents.

'On ye way to visit your auntie, I take it, Wee Tessa?'

'Aye, Mr. McTavish.' The little girl stood for a moment before glancing up shyly at the smiling farmer, plucking up the courage to ask him the burning question.

'Then you'd better be hurrying along then,' said the man. 'Ye don't want to be late,' he added in his deep, Scottish burr. He gave the silent child a puzzled look. 'Is there something else then?'

Tessa flushed a pretty pink before giving a shy, little smile. 'Can I ask you a very naughty question, please, Mr. McTavis?'

'Well now, that all depends on the question,' said the big man nervously, now aware that the little girl's gaze had dropped from his face and was instead focused on the area where his sporran would usually be.

'It's a very naughty question, Mr. McTavish!'

'Well, being a grownup I should think I've heard most naughty questions, young Tessa! '

The little face scrunched up again in concentration. 'Is it true that gentlemen wearing kilts don't wear anything underneath?' Little Tessa had now gone from pink to a bright red.

There was a stunned silence.

'Well, Mr. McTavish?' The curious, scrunched expression had now changed to a small frown.

'Quite true, wee Tessa. Quite true!' Now it was Ben McTavish's turn to start going red, his embarrassment mounting as if the little girl's gaze was actually <u>seeing</u> through the thick plaid fabric of his kilt.

Lifting her tiny face once more the little girl asked the question the big man was dreading. 'Can I please take a wee peek then, Mr. McTavish?'

'<u>What</u>?' The big man almost dropped the heavy post he had just picked up. Glancing anxiously around the empty, silent fields of basking heather, he gave a deep gulp. After all, he had children himself and his own little Flora had asked to see her daddy's wee wee only a few weeks back. 'Well, only a wee peek, then Tessa, lass.' And here the big man put on his most serious 'Daddy told you so,' expression. 'You don't say a word to ye auntie, mama or anyone, you hear? You must promise me that. Promise?'

'I promise,' said the little girl solemnly.

Big Ben McTavish quickly hoisted up the front of his heavy kilt before promptly dropping it, allowing Tessa only the briefest glimpse of his impressive – now somewhat aroused – uncut, thickset cock backed by a bloated pair of pendulous balls.

'Ooh!' exclaimed the now wide-eyed little girl, her eyes still riveted to the tartan fabric once more obscuring the object of her curiosity. 'It looks horrid! Rather like a big sausage and neeps!'

'It <u>is</u> a big sausage,' said the owner proudly. Feeling slightly embarrassed by his 'off-the-cuff performance,' he quickly added, 'Now you'd better run along like a good little girl, wee Tessa. And don't forget your promise!'

'What's his name?' questioned the little girl completely ignoring the suggestion.

'Er...Caber,' improvised Ben at a loss for anything else to say.

'Like in tossing the caber?' cried the little girl, followed by a tiny giggle.

'<u>Exactly</u>!' said Ben with a gulp. 'Exactly like a caber or big log.'

'Can I please just touch it?' asked the little angel, in all innocence. 'Does my friend Flora touch it?' she added.

Ben gave another gulp, his big, genial face beginning to redden. He glanced again nervously at the bight, purple fields of heather, empty apart from himself and the little girl.

'Err...yes, I mean no! Flora does <u>not</u> touch it!' He looked down at the pleading little face now peering up at his. 'Well, only a quick touch, Wee Tess! Nothing more! Here! Quickly! Up under my kilt!'

Taking a tiny step forward a tentative Tessa put her small arm under the thick kilt before wriggling her fingers as she felt for Caber, Ben making no attempt to lift the heavy fabric for her. He gave a sudden intake of breath as the little girl found the object of her curiosity and gave it more of a tug than a touch, then another, Caber responding an immediately to her determined little pulls.

'Ooh!' exclaimed wee Tessa, her hand recoiling from the feel of the soft warm foreskin as it retracted from the rapidly swelling, bulbous head. 'Ooh!' she exclaimed again, looking up aghast at the by now heavily breathing man. 'Caber's gruesome!'

Big Ben McTavish took a deeper gulp, Caber now beyond control. Screwing closed both his eyes the big man could only gasp hoarsely. 'If you want to feel again, Wee Tess, Caber's grew some more!'

A few moments later – after Tessa had happily obliged to do his bidding – the shuddering farmer managed to gasp, 'Ooh goodness, Wee Tess! You'd be a sure fire winner at the Highland Games in the Tossing The Caber section! End of story!'

'You dirty old sod!' shrieked Jenny, her massive bosoms jiggling with mirth. 'Now I suppose you both expect another drink or…' here she glanced at the silent little girl in the corner before adding in a giggled whisper, 'would you prefer *this* large lass to toss both *your* cabers instead?'

The evening of storytelling was to remain indelibly printed in young Morag's mind. A few years later, the plump but pretty teenager with her extraordinary skill at 'Tossing the Caber,' as she put it, was to become the hottest date in the village, her reputation even extending to several other neighbouring hamlets.

'Ask Morag out for a drink and get her to er… toss your caber, and you'll have never experienced anything like it before,' was the call of the day. Dedicated to the sport, the young woman became an avid visitor to any gathering where there was a *Tossing The Caber* competition. As the years quickly passed and Morag passed from young womanhood into middle age and then into her elderly years, she would sit entranced while watching her burly, kilted heroes lifting and throwing the mighty timber lengths, noting the perfect all-over loops and daintily cheering the sweaty, beefy, hirsute champions.

Most of her heroes had been boys from her childhood and teenage years, the majority of whose own cabers she had so joyfully tossed. Morag McClean never married but the silver-haired, gentle spinster remained treated with the highest respect – almost devotion – by these heroes.

Rory had never admitted to his being the initiator of her skills – the little girl having approached him several weeks later after hearing his telling of *Rory's Story*. Wee Morag had waited patiently until she was able to find the man alone. Her chance came one Sunday after church when – having plucked up enough courage – she waylaid the big man suitably kilted in his Sunday best and on the way to see *his* elderly aunt. This was another Sunday ritual for Rory before returning home to a typical family Sunday lunch.

It was a canny and devoted Morag who instigated her own very special version of 'tossing the caber' beginning with Rory's eldest, Andy, followed by his siblings Jamie, Robbie and inevitably all their friends and friends of friends.

At the funeral, a stooped, grey-haired Rory along with an array of devout array middle-aged male mourners, had all filed into the small stone church to pay their last respects to the little old lady, Rory's three sons and three of their friends were the pallbearers for the simple pine coffin.

All of these former protégés had come to the agreement that a plain, simple headstone would not suffice for their beloved Morag. Today Morag McClean sleeps peacefully beneath a splendid granite caber simply inscribed with the words 'Now it is our Morag's turn to be in the hands of God.'

LITTLE MISS MUFFIT

Dame Damara Despricable billed himself as a *Drag Queen Illusionist*, his slogan; 'What you see you believe; what you *don't* see your heart will *never* grieve.'

Dame Damara's stage was a seedy pub set in the nether regions of London's salubrious Fulham, close to the notorious 'coffin-cruisers' haven, the Brompton Cemetery. The pub, an old, solid Victorian building, built – according to a well-polished brass plaque – in 1850 and originally called *The Horse and Carriage* had, for some bizarre reason been renamed The Hindenburg by the last owner but one. 'Possibly the owner in the late thirties was some old queen whose fantasy was a cock in a condom, the size of the giant zeppelin!' was a joke much repeated by the regulars to curious visitors questioning the unusual name.

Over the years *The Hindenburg* had become a haven for a clientele comprising mainly of tired old queens who'd seen better years; bitchy young queens who never would; and a motley crowd of curious tourists who'd seen the pub listed in numerous 'freebie' gay magazines and papers as a place promising 'an evening of glamour and fun!'

Apart from being a regular 'name' in the adverts, Dame Damara's main claim to fame had been a feature in a pull-out colour supplement in one of the lesser Sunday tabloids. The article, titled '*Gay London Goes Gayer*', had seen a temporary increase in curious gays, curiosity seekers and groups of the usual swaggering 'look at me, I'm straight!' hecklers displaying both their ignorance and low IQ's.

Dame Damara's reference to these intruders was a sniffy, 'Ignorant, suppressed testosterone turds!' followed by a scathing 'they all secretly want it up the bum and then some! The more massive, the more passive! And usually their cock is a mock!'

Damara (the Dame can be dropped from now on) not only saw himself as an incarnate of Norma Desmond melded with Judy Garland but, thanks to a series of hyper-inflationary breast implants, a rival to Jessica Rabbit, the voluptuous heroine of Disney's '*Who Framed Roger Rabbit.*' It was inevitable that the name of the greatest femme fatale of them all, Mata Hari, would also have crossed his mind.

'Any man, I bet you *any* man – and he must be a man *man* – who walks into this place I can make mine! As dear Gwen Verdon sang in *Damn Yankees,* what *this* Lola wants, this Lola also gets!' was another favourite mantra.

'Pity the only thing our Lola gets is regularly pissed!' Betty, the hard-faced bartender would camp (Betty being a bitter forty year old failed actor, stage name Bryan Barrymore). 'I'm sure if that one ever saw a cock, hard or soft, she's run a mile! No – I sway corrected! – in those platforms make that hobble!'

'Quiet tonight, Bets,' said Ted, the bouncer, who, because of no drinkers at this early hour was sitting up at the bar enjoying a large rum and Coke while generally boring Betty about his latest (fantasy) conquests.

'This one's for keeps, Bets,' he'd been telling him before Damara's impending arrival.

'Yeah, keep for a week and then she'll keep away!' camped Betty.

'Tart!' said Ted, his fleshy lips broadening into a loose smile, 'And I'll have another of these if you don't mind!'

'Takes one to know one!' said Betty crisply, pouring a healthy dollop of rum into a clean glass and topping it up from the relevant hose. Giving Ted a lewd wink he added, 'After all this talk, isn't it about time, Ted, you showed us girls what you've really got beneath that belly of yours? Big brute like you either has a whopper of a chopper or a midget digit! We're all *dying* to find out!'

'I'll have to send you a wreath then!' chuckled Ted, ''Cause all you desperate queens'll die before you find out!'

Betty glanced at a door partly hidden in the shadows to the side of the bar. 'Oh, oh, here she comes, the Grande Dame of Failure! Her nibs Dame Damara Despricable in all her tatty glory! Evening Damara, the usual?'

'No thank you, Elizabeth,' said Damara in his strangled contralto-like voice. Giving what he considered a throaty, seductive chuckle (more of a gargle) he added, 'Tonight I feel in a *wanton* mood and when I'm in the thrall of being wanton I don't need the stimulation of even the remotest alcoholic libation to pass my lips!'

'Yeah, *wanton* and never gettin',' sniggered Ted.

'I heard that, Ted!' snapped Damara, dark eyes narrowing under their heavy diamante lashes. Drawing himself to his full height six foot height (five foot six inches in reality plus six inches of platform heels). 'Just because I have never, ever been attracted to a brutish lout – a Neanderthal if I may say so – like yourself, there is no need to be so vindictive and vacuous at the same time!'

'Ooh! 'Ark at 'er!' laughed Ted, affecting a bad East End accent, crudely adding, 'My cock's very choosy, Damara! 'E only goes for proper front fanny, not backroom granny!'

'Up yours!' said Damara graciously.

'No way, Dame Damara Despricable! What you secretly hanker for is me cock goin' *up yours*!'

'Now, now you two!' cut in Betty, slightly alarmed at the bitchy scene gathering momentum in front of him. 'Calm down you two! Damara, may I suggest a Harlow Stinger, on the house, *despite* your wanton mood!'

'Sounds about right, a harlot stringer!' quipped Ted, hardening the T and rolling the Rs.

'I said shut it Ted!'

'Will do, will do!' grinned Ted, 'though I doubt Damara could, judging from all the successes she claims to have had!'

'I'll ignore such vulgarity,' hissed Damara, raising his several chins, his bright red Madge Simpson-styled wig (and an extra fifteen inches) vibrating with indignation. 'Elizabeth, if you don't mind, I'll have my Harlow Stinger over at my usual table, the *star's* table, where I know the company will be more conducive to my present mood.'

'If yer wantin' you won't be gettin' sittin' in the dark all by yourself. Unnoticed!'

Damara glared imperiously at the grinning man. 'You're beneath contempt!' he breathed haughtily.

'Yeah, like anything beneath that hairdo is exempt!' chortled Ted.

'Enough, Ted!' said Betty sharply, trying to stifle a laugh. 'Now Damara, you take yourself over to the star's table like the lovely legend you are and I'll bring over Miss Harlow to join you. Maybe the two of you can sit and reminisce before you have to face the cheering crowds!'

'Thank you, Elizabeth,' said Damara graciously before teetering over to the aforesaid table nestling in the gloom.

'You are awful Ted,' giggled Betty, 'sending the poor old thing up like that!'

'Stupid old relic! Why doesn't she just put herself out to grass? She's already gone to seed so it shouldn't be too difficult!'

'Ted!'

'Tell you what, Bets,' – the big man leant forward conspiratorially – 'Want to see a bit of fun?'

'Yeees,' Betty's 'yes' was cautious, he was well aware of Ted's personal jokes, most of which were more vindictive as opposed to funny.

'I think the old bag is secretly pissed off because I've never made a pass for 'er arse!'

'But you're *straight,* Ted!' exclaimed Betty, feigning surprise.

'Ah, but "desperate stokes for desperate folks" as me old mum used to say! And I 'ave to confess I 'ave used the old back entrance on the very odd occasion; me good deed for the day so to speak. Make some poor old soul happy.' Ted gave a lewd laugh followed by a leer and sly wink. 'But it's not often, I must admit, I get a tan on me prick!'

'That's *disgusting*, Ted!'

'I am, aren't I?' said the big man proudly, pushing his glass forward for a refill. 'So, what d'ya say?'

'To what?'

'Shall I give it a go? See if I can seduce the world's oldest *femme fatale*? Seduce Methuselah's great grandma?'

Betty gave a toss of a lank, bleached lock of hair. 'You wouldn't dare!'

'Try me! I bet you another large rum and Coke she'll be *ready to go* right after her show!'

'You're on!'

Draining his last glass, Ted took up his current refill – the winning refill still to follow – and ambled over to the lone figure sitting stiff backed in the darkened corner.

'Damara, may I join you?'

'Why?'

'Because I'd like to and also, I'd like to apologize. I was a bit out of order earlier!'

'A bit?' Damara gave a sneer, his lips (the same colour as her Madge Simpson wig) wriggling like a giant red caterpillar across his heavily powdered face. He reached for his sequined evening bag. 'Somehow I don't think so!'

'Oh, c'mon, Damara! It's this place; all these queens and their never-ending bitching, it gets to you after a while.'

'Well, it's certainly gotten to *you*! If it came to a degree in bitchery, venom and vitriol you'd pass with flying colours!'

'Please?' Ted gave what he considered his most soulful and remorseful look.

'Oh, alright then!' Damara looked up with surprise as Betty arrived carrying a tray bearing another Harlow Stinger plus large rum and Coke. 'It's a peace offering,' grinned the barman, 'and Ted's buying, even though he didn't know it!'

'Thank you, Elizabeth and thank you too, Ted!' said Damara graciously, taking the proffered drink in his large, multi-ringed hand.

'My pleasure,' said Ted, giving Damara what he considered his most charming smile, a twist of his lips most people would have regarded as a sneer.

The two sat sipping their drinks in an uncomfortable silence before Ted, giving another showing of his special smile, said quietly, 'Damara, there's something I need to tell you. You know the old saying, *the lady doth protest too much*? Well, that's me! And though I'm no lady' – here the big man gave a deep belly laugh – 'I have been protesting too much! You see, Damara, I really fancy you but I've been too shy to say so! Hence all me leg-pulling an' bitchiness!'

'Tosh!' said Damara, although the unladylike 'bullshit' would have been preferable.

'Oh, but I do! Ask Betty!'

'I wouldn't ask Betty for a penny,' said Damara haughtily, although the unladylike 'a lost fart in a thunderstorm' would have, again, been even more preferable.

'Oh dear,' said Ted, putting on a woebegone expression. 'I just *knew* you'd be like this! Although I have a massive cock, I also know I'm ugly, hideously ugly – like the Incredible Hulk on a bad day, but that doesn't stop me from having feelings, you know?'

The two magic words, massive and cock, had sparked off the desired effect, Damara feeling a sudden long forgotten tingling of the neurons! 'I'm sorry,' he said, making a moue (another violent caterpillar movement) with his vibrant lips 'Forgive my brusqueness. But I always get first night nerves before a show, even after all my years in show business.' Here he gave a self-deprecating laugh. 'They say that the first time you *don't* get a touch of the old first night syndrome, you're a goner!'

'I'm feeling a bit like that.'

'What? A goner?'

'No, first night nerves!' Ted cleared his throat volubly, 'I'd really like to fuck you, you know?'

'Well really!' An indignant Damara, gathering up his evening bag, clambered inelegantly to his feet where he stood swaying precariously on his platform heels. 'I am an *artiste,* mister! Not a whore! And don't you ever forget it!' With that Damara made as if to turn away.

'How can I forget you're an *artiste* and how can I forget *you*?' came the humbled voice from the shadows. 'And what is more important is how I can ever expect you to forget and forgive *me*?'

'My dressing room downstairs, after the show,' moued Damara again. With a fluttering of his enormous diamante eyelashes he teetered away leaving a grinning Ted to emerge from the shadows to give an equally grinning Betty the thumbs up sign.

Damara, gold lamé gloved arms outstretched, bowed deeply and graciously, modestly accepting the thunderous applause (a party of six young very drunken gays plus two gloomy-looking couples – it was, after all, a rainy Monday night in dreariest Fulham). Walking proudly from the dingy stage, his head held high, the lonely figure teetered down the narrow cement steps and along a dingy, ill lit corridor to his isolated basement dressing room.

Sitting in front of the chipped, flyblown theatrical-style mirror, Damara sat staring at his lurid reflection and then again at the cheap sealed envelope leaning against an almost used up jar of cold cream; five simple words 'To Whom It May Concern' printed on the envelope in his wavering hand.

Checking the contents of the black lacquer jewel box (a souvenir from a visit to St Petersburg where he had found himself playing Lara to a vigorous Russian Zhivago) Damara gave a long sigh before saying softly to the reflection, 'Well Ted, what an unfortunate choice of an evening you've made.'

A muffled knock on the heavy door followed by an almost inaudible, 'Your shy stallion arrives!' broke Damara from his reverie.

'Oh Ted, you silly, silly man,' whispered Damara to the pale reflection, more Kabuki doll than human. 'Coming,' he crooned (he couldn't coo due to the thickness of the old Victorian door), 'Coming!'

'Hopefully that'll soon be me!' came the suggestive, muffled laugh, followed by an impatient rattling of the door knob.

Damara, wincing at the coarseness of the reply, slipped on a pair of pink, marabou trimmed mules and made his way wearily over to the door. 'Coming!' he crooned slightly louder. Unbolting the door he pulled it open, striking his best Mae West pose. 'Glad you decided to come *down* and see me some time?' he said in his strangulated contralto.

'I've brought as a bottle of champagne,' said Ted, beaming proudly, producing a bottle of cheap, sweet Italian sparkling wine from behind his broad back (This being sold by the glass in the pub as their best champagne).

'What a way to go,' murmured Damara.

'Snug in here,' observed Ted, looking round the small, cluttered tomb-like dressing room.

'I like it,' said Damara, collecting two wine glasses from a small tray table. 'Hidden away in the basement – it used to be a wine cellar – it's a perfect place to relax after a performance, so quiet and so peaceful. You don't hear a sound.' Damara gave a throaty laugh, 'And that is why I have two clocks plus a watch and I keep an eye on each! I dread being late for my entrance – not that I ever have, oh no, not Dame Damara Despricable! Never ever! I mean, a star can become absorbed in a novel or a magazine – we are human, after all – so that's my motto, keep an eye on the cock!'

Ted blinked, not quite sure as to whether he'd heard 'cock' or 'clock' but assumed the latter. 'Of course, shall I do the honours?'

'Champagne flutes are over there,' said Damara, pointing to the two wine glasses which, alongside the lacquer box, had now been placed on the low coffee table in front of the small sofa. 'And please, pray do be seated.' Perching himself on the sagging sofa Damara patted the faded cushion alongside him. A few seconds later Ted lowered himself down alongside, causing what were left of the original sofa springs to complain alarmingly.

'Is it really that big, Ted?' asked Damara.

Completely taken by surprise the big man gave a gulp, 'Well, err... yes'

'I have a weird obsession, almost a kinkiness,' murmured Damara, fluttering the glittering eyelids and giving Ted an eerie doll-like stare with his dark eyes.

'Err... and what's that, then?' said Ted, giving a nervous swallow while thinking, Christ! In this light she's more like Dracula's grandma than Methuselah's. Talk about fucking spooky. I'll give the old bag a quick fuck and then fuck on right out of here!

'Before I allow myself to be possessed err... so as to fulfill the desires of virile studs like yourself, I first request that my possessor-to-be strip himself and sit alongside me, naked.'

'You're joking?'

'No, asking.'

'You want me to strip off all my gear and then sit down here next to you, stark bullock naked?'

'Yes please, Teddy Bear!'

'Shit!' said Ted going a deep crimson but chuffed by the term 'Teddy Bear.' Being covered with a thick coating of body hair the big man had been called Teddy Bear by a shrieking young queen or two – plus the occasional lady – on numerous occasions. 'OK then,' he said with a fleshy smile, 'but then you are going to allow me to err... possess you?'

'It will be an honour!'

A few moments later Ted, naked apart from his orange ankle socks was again sitting alongside Damara who, in turn, sat daintily holding his wine glass, the bottle along with the lacquer box on the table in front of the two.

'Well, what do you think?' asked Ted proudly.

'I can't see very much under that enormous, hairy Hanging Gardens of Babylon of stomach,' said Damara cuttingly.

'Hold on,' said Ted encircling his vast, hirsute gut with an equally large pair of hirsute arms and, with an almost Herculean effort, hoisted the large flabby mass up towards his chest.

'Heavens!' exclaimed Damara looking at the long, thick flaccid, uncircumcised cock flopped down over the sofa's edge. 'Heavens,' he said again, eyelashes glittering, 'Impressive, most impressive! What are you, even like that? Eight?'

'It gets bigger and much, much fatter,' said Ted proudly, 'at least another two to two and a half inches!'

'Well then, there's only one way to prove you point,' said Damara. 'Give it a rub!' Giving another coquettish glance he added, 'Like that naughty nursery rhyme, full of innuendo; *Rub a dud dub, three men in a tub*! I mean, just what were those three men doing rubbing each other up in a tub?'

'Ah, naughty nursery rhymes,' said Ted with a grin. 'Why Damara, I can almost see you as *Mary, Mary, not quite so unwary*!'

'Ah yes Teddy, and how does *your garden grow*?'

Ted gave a leer as he began to move his heavy foreskin (unfortunately slightly rancid) back and forth, '*With pretty inches all in a row*!' he chuckled, his cock beginning to harden, forming a thick, formidable bulbous club.

'Another one for you,' grunted Ted, his face taking on a deeper flush, his large, ham-like hand beginning to pump faster. 'This could easily apply to that table of little queens upstairs!' Now sweating profusely and causing Damara to wrinkle his powdered nose at Ted's pungent body odour, the big man continued, his speech quickening, '*Georgie Porgie Pudding and Pie, he kissed the boys and made 'em cry! His mother said, you dreadful child, you'll grow up just like Oscar Wilde*!'

'How about *Little Miss Muffit*?' laughed Damara.

'How about *Little Miss Muffit*?' gasped Ted, his exertions about to come to an unprecedented climax.

'*Little Miss Muffit*' began Damara, leaning surreptitiously towards the lacquer box, '*Little Miss Muffit, she sat on her tuffet, her panties all tattered and torn, it wasn't a spider that sat down beside her but little Boy Blue and his horn*!'

'What about Ted's horn?' gasped the big man, his cock ready to explode.

'How *about* Ted's horn?' hissed Damara, snatching a gleaming scalpel from the lacquer box and severing Ted's cock from below where it was gripped in his hand. Suddenly released from his groin Ted's hand – along with his severed cock – flew up into the air, hitting the wall behind with a resounding thud.

Ted's wild screams of pure terror went unheard in the depth of the secluded basement room, only to be silenced by Damara deftly severing Ted's fleshy throat.

Slowly the blood spattered man returned to his seat in front of the dressing table mirror. 'Now your turn, dear,' said Damara to the blood speckled pale reflection. *'This poor Little Bo Peep, she's certainly lost all her sheep...'*

With a sigh, Damara Despricable, the legend who never was, determinedly slashed his wrists.

PETER, THE PERFIDIOUS PLUMBER

'Bloody tap! Drip! Drip! Drip! Talk about fucking Chinese water torture! This, Calpurnia, is driving me out of my *skull*!'

Crispin glared at the Siamese cat whose matching blue eyes stared back uncomprehendingly.

'Oh, well fine! Look at me like that if you must!' camped her young master, 'and I'm sorry if I offended your feline sensitivities by saying Chinese instead of Siamese!' Giving out a high pitched giggle Crispin couldn't resist adding, 'but somehow *Siamese* water torture doesn't somehow have the same meow!'

Giving Crispin a contemptuous glance Clapurnia merely stuck up one leg and proceeded to busily clean herself with her long, raspy tongue.

'Rude cunt!' sniped Crispin giving the cat an affectionate stroke on her bobbing head. 'Now where did I put that card?' he murmured, a thin, delicate finger placed lightly on his pale, dimpled chin. Foraging through an assortment of business cards tossed carelessly over a period of time into one of the kitchen drawers, he finally found the one in question, a card picked up at random in a gay pub.

'Ah yes,' he said to a disinterested Calpurnia, still busily washing herself. *'Peter the Plumber* 'he read out loud, *'Qualified and quick! Let Peter handle any plumbing problems! Emergency callouts at any hour!* Hmm, I suppose he *is* a bona fide plumber,' mused Crispin. 'Though, reading between the lines it could be a cover up for an escort prepared to *plumb* any depths!' With a snigger, he continued, 'Well, there's only one way to find out; let's ring him and see!' Picking up the portable phone he dialed the relevant number. After a few ring the call was answered by a deep, cheery voice, 'Peter the plumber, qualified and quick, how may I help you?'

'Err… Peter, you *are* a qualified plumber, I take it?' I mean, I'm not being rude but I did pick up your card in The Star…'

'I'm a *very* proper plumber, sir!' came the quick reply, 'and being gay myself I prefer to advertise in gay venues.' The deep voice gave a friendly chuckle, 'I believe looking after the gay fraternity to the best of my plumbing abilities and *not* in any adverse way! Now, how can I help you?'

'Well,' said Crispin, flushing slightly with embarrassment at Peter's slight reprimand, 'it's nothing life threatening, simply a dripping kitchen tap,' – he gave a self-conscious giggle – 'but as I was just saying to Calprunia it's getting to be rather like the Siamese water torture!'

'Siamese water torture?'

Oh, silly me! I meant *Chinese* water torture! It's all Calpurnia's fault!'

'Sorry, I'm getting a bit confused here. What has this err… Calpurnia got to do with your dripping faucet?'

'Oh,' giggled Crispin, not too sure as to whether the mysterious Peter's reply was a deliberate double entendre or not, 'Calpurnia's my cat! She's a Siamese, hence all the confusion, you see…'

'Not exactly but leaving Calpurnia out of this now I know she's innocent, let's get back to your dripping faucet or tap. This is in the kitchen, you say?'

'Yes, it's the cold water tap. It's driving me *mad* with its drip, drip, drip!'

'Well, we can't have this continuing sir.' There was a pause. 'Your name and address?'

'Oh, Crispin Clegg and the flat's in Cadogan Gardens.' Here Crispin rattled off the street and flat number, adding dramatically, 'You say *we* can't have this continuing! Does this mean it could be dangerous?' Not giving the man a chance to reply he quickly went on. 'You couldn't come round like say, this morning, could you? It's only I'm out of the country as from tonight on a photo shoot. I could be away for several days or more.' Crispin gave a small gasp. 'I dread, simply *dread* the idea of coming back to a flooded flat!'

Peter gave another laugh, 'Even if I couldn't get round today, Mr. Clegg, unless you leave the plug in the sink, I don't see your drip, drip, drip becoming a major disaster! I'm sure you'd make sure the plug wasn't inserted before you left, wouldn't you?'

'Of course I would!' snorted Crispin, 'but I must say that even while I've been talking to you I seem to be dripping faster!'

'Now that *does* sound serious, Mr. Clegg, if talking to me is activating your dripping! How about if get there in an hour? It's just gone nine and I can be with you my ten at the latest.' There was a soft chuckle, 'In fact, it's most convenient as my next appointment is in Egerton Crescent at eleven.'

'Oh, so you'll be that quick?' camped Crispin.

'If, as you say it's only a dripping faucet, I'll be that quick!' came the laughing reply. 'And by the way, Mr. Clegg, my rates are a hundred pounds an hour which I prefer in cash.' There was a short pause. 'If I have to accept a cheque there is an additional charge of twenty per cent making it a hundred and twenty pounds.'

'Oh, that much?' murmured Crispin.

'Mr. Clegg,' came the terse response, 'I am sure there are other emergency plumbers you can ring. Otherwise, simply keep yourself unplugged and find someone else on your return.'

'Oh no! It simply has to be *you* Peter, as you've already been so considerate and obliging,' simpered Crispin. 'No, cash is fine, I've got a stash here which I was going to change into Euros at the airport but then, I can always use a credit card in Prague, if I'm caught short.'

'Then I look forward to seeing you and err… Calpurnia at ten, Mr. Clegg,' confirmed the rich, deep voice.

'Me too!' giggled Crispin coquettishly, now totally convinced Peter the plumber, from his voice, as either doppelgänger to butch Burt Reynolds in his *Deliverance* days or even better, a more up-to-date craggy Daniel Craig. 'And Peter, Crispin per-lease as opposed to Mr. Clegg! Much more pink pound!' he added with a trill.

Helping himself to another cup of coffee, Crispin turned to Calpurnia now deeply engrossed in cleaning her long tail. 'We've a big, butch, macho visitor in a few minutes, Miss Calpurnia,' he cooed, 'so I want you on your best behaviour, please! No rubbing yourself or pushing and purring against legs, thank you, which, from the sound of his voice, can only be more tree trunks than twigs!'

Humming to himself Crispin moved through to his bedroom. Taking of his Hermes bathrobe he sashayed on to the en suite bathroom where he took a quick shower, soaping himself generously with a sandalwood-scented soap. Having shaved, he smoothed a moisturiser onto his face before added a hint of blusher to his cheeks. Satisfied with his lightly bronzed appearance he made a deft application of a roll-on deodorant to his shaven armpits. Blow drying his long blond hair and suitably mussing this up into a carefree, casual look he blew his reflection a kiss before returning to the bedroom. Slipping into a pair of loose-fitting chinos, he pulled on a T shirt and sprayed himself liberally with Gucci *Pour Homme* before finally slipping on a pair of suede Gucci loafers.

Waltzing back into the kitchen Crispin gave a pirouette in front of a dozing Calpurnia. 'How do I look?' he trilled, spinning round once more and coming face to face with the tall fridge freezer. 'And why not?' he questioned out loud. 'Obviously we'll all be pissed by the time we board our flight this afternoon so who's counting?'

Taking out a bottle of champagne plus one of Stolichnaya, he quickly opened both, pouring a fifty- fifty mix into a large wine glass.

'Delicious,' he murmured, having taken a large, satisfying sip. Sitting himself at the small, circular glass and steel breakfast table he eyed the cat who returned his gaze through half closed eyes. 'Will you miss me, Calpurnia, *dear*?' he cooed. 'However, I very much doubt it, you fickle female you! Anyway, mad Magda from upstairs has promised to drop by and check on you, keep you fed and watered and also, bless her, change your litter tray if necessary. Hopefully you'll be tactful enough to use the other tray on the kitchen balcony.' Crispin took another sip before sticking out his tongue at the silent cat back to eyeing him with a baleful stare. 'So much for gratitude,' he sniped, reaching for his itinerary for the next few days. 'Cat got your tongue?' he added still staring at the silent animal. *'Cat got your tongue?* Oh, I'm such a wit!' he shrieked, adding with a champagne and vodka infused giggle, 'I don't quite know how I manage to live with myself! Which reminds me I'd better leave a little *reminder* note for Magda.'

Reaching for a notepad emblazoned with the words *NO SHIT* he quickly scribbled, *'Magda, darling! If you notice silence is golden it's because I've finally had the drip fixed I Ha Ha, and I don't me MOI! Thanks again for looking after C. I've left six cans of cat's fodder on the counter under the electric can opener – all mod cons for this princess! – and simply*

change the water in her bowl for madam, as you know, does not drink milk!
The litter tray should not be a problem as it's the one on the kitchen balcony
she seems to favour! See you when I'm back which could be next week
(supposedly Thursday!), or maybe the week after or maybe never at all!
Who knows, I may even meet my 'Czech mate' in passionate Prague and live
happily fucked every after! xx CRISP xx'

At ten o'clock precisely the intercom buzzer sounded. Emboldened
by a third large glass of vodka and champagne Crispin answered with a
camp, '*Hello* plumber!' before letting Peter in through the main door to the
building.

Opening his own front door he stood waiting for the lift carrying his
guest up to the third floor. Leaning provocatively against the door jamb, he
gave an anticipatory smile for the about to arrive Burt or Daniel lookalike,
his smile faltering at another possibility. 'My God!' he muttered as the lift
came to a stop, 'what if he's all voice and no vice and I end up with Henri
Toulouse Lautrec? Oh!' Crispin gave an audible sigh as a combination of
Messrs Reynolds and Craig stepped from the lift.

'Crispin?' said the tall, smiling man, holding out a brawny hand,
a large canvas tool bag in the other. 'I'm Peter, your plumber and bang on
time!'

'Well, hello Peter!' cooed Crispin, his mind racing. But he's *gorgeous*
and if he *is* a bona fide plumber, what a *waste*! (The double entendre being
completely overlooked) 'Come in,' he added, feeling more Mata Hari than
ever, 'and I'll introduce you to the instigator of my call!'

'Nice flat,' commented Peter, eyeing a large modernistic-looking
sitting room on his left as he followed the sashaying young man through the
elegant Art Deco-styled entrance hall.

'Thank you,' simpered Crispin, 'my little haven away from it all! The
culprit's through here,' he added, flinging open the door to show a gleaming,
modern kitchen. Pointing dramatically at the sink he hissed theatrically –
and to Peter, obviously drunkenly – 'There she is, Farah faucet, our major
problem! Oh,' he added with a shriek, turning to the bemused man, 'Forgive
me! Just a slip of the tongue' I'm *such* a fan – or was – and of course I still
adore Lee!'

Noticing Peter eyeing the two bottles and the half-filled glass he
added, 'A little morning libation before heading for the airport. The team
and I are off to Prague this afternoon for a fashion shoot.'

'So you said,' mused Peter, changing his gaze from the glass to his own booted feet, 'and this, I take it, doing her best to trip me up, must be the much maligned Calpurnia?'

'Maligned? More manipulative than maligned!' trilled Crispin. 'Do excuse her!' Giving a slight stumble he stooped to pick up the cat from where she was rubbing herself against Peter's jeans and purring loudly. 'She can be such a tart when there's a new man in the house! Not that there're that many!' he added with a giggle. 'But Peter, you must think me *hideously* rude not offering you a drink, so please, something before you start? I'm drinking White Bear, a mixture of champers and vodka. Would you care for a glass of that or don't you believe in drinking while plumbing?' Crispin's reaction to this bon mot being a high pitched shriek.

'I drink, plumb and drive,' laughed the big, brawny, genial man. 'So, Crispin, if you please, pop it there on the draining board and I'll get started.' Smiling at the young man as he fumbled for another glass in one of the cupboards, Peter added, 'I'll need to turn this section of the water off so perhaps you can show me your stopcock?'

Magda looked at the note, a smile playing on her heavily painted lips. 'Silly queen,' she muttered, 'I hadn't even *noticed* a dripping tap!' Lifting a tin of cat food she pressed the top to the electric opener. Removing the lid she quickly spooned the contents into an empty, pink ceramic bowl, the name Calpurnia painted on it in gold, then placed the bowl down alongside its twin containing water. 'No doubt that's fresh from this morning so *that* can wait until tomorrow,' she said aloud, glancing round the kitchen. 'Now, where's the bloody cat?'

Having peered vaguely into the sitting room she made her way back to the kitchen where, after a few self-conscious calls of 'pussy, pussy, here pussy,' Magda shrugged her shoulders saying, 'Well, be like that, cat!' imagining the animal to have gone through the cat flap and was somewhere on the balcony.

Closing the front door behind her Magda pressed for the lift to take her back up to her flat on the fifth floor. Two days later she had to admit to herself 'something must have happened to the bloody thing!' the comment made on seeing the bowl of food untouched. Wrinkling her nose, Magda threw the contents down the waste disposal, rinsed the bowl and set down a fresh bowl of cat food along with a bowl of replacement water. By the following Thursday she was bracing herself for Crispin's return. As she had often said to Diana, her partner in the exclusive interior design company the two owned, 'If Crispin wasn't so obviously gay I would have sworn, for sure, he was having an affair with the bloody creature!'

'Bloody cat,' she muttered as she rinsed out the bowl on Thursday morning, 'All this yummy food wasted!' adding with a grin, 'Obviously bloody Madam Calpurnia doesn't give a cat's whisker for all those starving alley cats out there!'

Back at the design offices a few days later – Magda having given up putting out any more food or bothering to check Crispin's flat – she turned to Diana, the two sitting having their de rigueur mid-morning glass of wine, saying, 'Di, don't you think it a bit odd Crispin hasn't called? I mean, he surely would have let me, or you – he adores chatting to you – know if he was going to be away longer than his scheduled week?'

'Are you sure he isn't back and simply hasn't popped by to let you know. I mean, poor darling does work in one of the most frenetic businesses!'

'I haven't really noticed. It's just he did say last Thursday but then again, nothing specific' Magda gave a hollow laugh. 'It's that damned missing cat I'm more worried about!'

'I wouldn't worry about the cat, nine lives and all that!' Diana gave a laugh, 'Maybe he *has* found true love in Prague?'

'He wishes!'

'Anyway, as I said, all those people involved in the fashion trade are completely unreliable! Now, what are we going to do about this bloody Carter woman? Talk about a client from hell!'

Several evenings after her discussion with Diana, Magda answered the main front door intercom to a young man introducing himself as Paul, a colleague of Crispin's from the fashion agency.

'I'm here with another colleague, Miss De La Rue,' he explained, 'we're all worried about Crisp – I mean Crispin. We found your address in his book and, as it's the same building…'

'Come up,' instructed Magda. 'Take the lift to the third floor and I'll meet you there. I have a key to the flat.' She gave a sigh, 'Now you've really got me worried.'

'We have?'

'Yes, because his cat's gone missing as well!'

Apart from a few letters lying inside the front door, the flat was eerily silent. 'When did *you* get back?' questioned Magda, now deeply concerned.

'*We* got back last Thursday, Miss De La Rue,' said Paul, pointing to Stephanie, his blonde companion. 'Crispin never made the airport for when we *left*! We've texted him, sent emails and left messages but zilch! Nothing!'

'But how extraordinary!' exclaimed Magda. 'He left me a note with some piddling instructions – damn! I threw it out – about leaving food and water for Calpurnia, that's the cat, which I repeatedly did but it was obvious the cat hasn't been around as the food was never touched.' She looked at the two anxious faces staring back at her. 'What do you think we should do?' she added lamely.

'Does he have any family you know of?' asked Paul.

'Not that I know of.' Magda gave a small smile. 'Crispin was simply a fun neighbour even though a bit of an enigma. But surely you, or the organization, office whatever, must have some details or contacts?'

'None whatsoever. Crispin worked freelance, so we have no details,' cut in Stephanie.

'Do you suppose we report him missing?' asked Magda. 'I simply have no idea what the procedure is in such matters. After all, it's not as if we're family or anything like that?'

'Let's give it until next Monday and if he's not turned up, *then* we go to the police,' suggested Paul.

'I agree,' said a relieved Magda.

'Me too,' said Stepahanie.

It was a week to the day, the police having been informed, PC Rivers along with PC Lake, on an initial visit to Crispin's flat, inadvertently opened the doors to the tall fridge to find Crispin's naked, frozen body stuffed inside, the temperature having been set on its coldest. A later search had shown the interior shelving from the fridge neatly stacked inside the broom cupboard. It was obvious any perishables had been either taken away or put down the waste disposal. Another puzzlement were the finger prints found within the flat, these belonging either to Crispin, Magda or Mrs. Summers, Crispin's cleaner who, at the time of his disappearance, was on a two weeks holiday staying with her sister in Cornwall.

An autopsy showed Crispin as having been brutally fucked before having his cock and balls viciously sawn off with a serrated instrument similar to a hacksaw and stuffed down his throat, choking him to death. Due to the perpetrator of the crime wearing both gloves and a condom, no DNA evidence was possible.

While details of *'The Body in the Fridge'* livened up the tabloids for a few days, the demise of Crispin Clegg was soon forgotten and nobody else, apart from the original three, Madga, Paul and Stepahnie, made any enquiries about the missing young man.

During one of her interviews with the police Magda had brought up the possible visit of a plumber, a lead which was to go nowhere.

THREE MONTHS LATER:

Derek Miller dialed the number from the card picked up randomly from one of the many gay pubs he frequented. 'Peter the plumber,' answered a deep, resonant voice, 'qualified and quick! How may I help?'

'Oh, err... Peter, yes, I hope so! I need to run an extension feed for a new ornamental pond I'm planning for my small terrace. Can you help?'

'I'm sure I can help you with an extension feed,' came the reply followed by a few muffled mumblings.

'Sorry, I missed that, err... Peter.'

'No, my fault entirely,' came the deep, rich laughing reply. 'I was just speaking to Calpurnia, my cat, she's always curious when I'm talking on the phone!'

'Oh,' came the camp reply, 'I shouldn't say it but curiosity *killed* the cat!'

'Not only the cat!' laughed Peter. 'Now sir, your name and address, please. Well, there's a coincidence, I have an appointment quite near there tomorrow afternoon so I could call by later so as to have a look and give you a quote. Would six o'clock be convenient?'

'That would be divine!' crooned Derek, adding with a giggle, 'the ornamental pond's a birthday treat from me to myself!'

'Yourself? Oh, Mr. Miller, I don't believe it, surely you will be getting a load more presents?

'No, just me to me and tomorrow is the actual day.'

'Don't tell me you're going to be alone on your birthday?'

'Ah, but I am! Footloose and fancy free, that's me!' came the light-hearted reply.

'Well, I tell you what, Mr. Miller...'

'Derek, per-lease!'

'I tell you what, Derek, I'll bring along a bottle of wine – a bottle from me and Calpurnia – and we'll drink a lucky toast to your birthday; Calpurnia being *my* lucky mascot!'

'How *sweet!*' squealed Derek. 'Err… Peter,' he gave a small giggle, 'A *lucky* cat? I take it she's not a black cat then?'

'Oh no! You're not superstitious are you, Derek?'

'Oh no, Peter! Not at all! I love cats, all cats! I was only being funny ha ha, not funny peculiar!' Derek gave our another giggle, more coquettish this time, 'I love anything beginning with the word cat; like shopping catalogues, various categories' – here there was a deliberate pause before he added mischievously – 'maybe even cat-o-nine-tails?'

'Cat-o-nine tails, Derek?' repeated Peter with a chuckle, 'Now *that* cat, if one's not careful, could lead to a catastrophe!'

'Ah, but like a cat I'm sure I'm blessed with nine lives!' giggled Derek Miller.

'I look forward to meeting lucky you tomorrow then!' laughed Peter before clicking off the phone and bending to stroke a purring Calpurnia.

WHAT PASSES FOR A SMILE

Phillip checked his teeth in the brightly lit bathroom mirror, 'If turd yellow is the new white I'm OK,' he muttered, 'but if it isn't, then I'm in even deeper shit than the colour of my fangs!' Setting aside the electric toothbrush he gave his mouth a quick rinse of Corsadil Daily. 'Bugger,' he said to his bronzed reflection, 'I hate to admit it but Toby's right, fine for the model shots but as for the teeth? No, something has to be done and *tout de suite*!'

Walking through to his stylish sitting room – sofas from Kingcome, mirrored tables from Andrew Martin – Phillip picked up the telephone. 'Morning Tobes, me. OK, you win,' he said with a shit-coloured grimace 'You know I'd almost prefer having to face – God forbid! – an evil, odious, hairy cunt rather than a bloody dentist but you're right, no amount of air brushing will compensate for the real thing seeing I will soon have to fucking well *smile* in public. So, who *is* this medieval torturer you so cruelly recommend?'

'John Armstrong. He's great. One of the best.'

'Is he expensive?'

'Jesus Phil, as I keep telling you there is no such thing as *cheap and cheerful*! Do it on the cheap and you always end up in the shit!'

'Rather like my teeth,' sniggered Phillip.

'To put it bluntly, Phil – no pun intended – *exactly* like your teeth!'

'Charming,' muttered Phillip.

'I'll get Liz to call him now. Any particular day or time?'

'Let's get the fucker over with, the sooner the better.' Phillip slumped down into a Charles Eames   chair. 'If he could do me Friday that'd be great.' He gave a snigger. 'I've a hot date this weekend so I'll now be able to give him a double flash to remember!'

'Anyone *we* know?'

'No, Tobes, no one we know! Someone advertising on the internet if *you* must know!'

'You're not advertising yourself on the internet are you?' came the startled response.

'Of course not, you idiot! I rather enjoy the reaction when, on meeting yours truly, the guy finds out he's actually meeting Phillip de Silva, the mean, macho man, the face behind the clothes and toiletries for *Pantastic.*'

'So be it. And Phillip.'

'Toby?'

'Rather fortuitous you deciding to do this.'

'Oh, and why is that?' asked Phillip smiling yellowly to himself in anticipation of Toby's reply.

'*Pantastic* is planning on bringing out a new toothpaste and mouthwash in their *Pantastic Pour Homme* range. Your timing to have your teeth seen to could not have been more perfect.' Toby gave a small snigger. 'Their advertising department has already asked for some shots of you *smiling*! OK, we could have got away with touching these up.' The snigger became more of a chuckle. 'Uncanny isn't it? In the past you've been portrayed as the stern-faced guy staring moodily from all your shots and now they're planning on using you and a new slogan, something along the lines of *Pantastic makes even Phillip de Silva Smile!*'

'Shit!'

'My thoughts exactly,' laughed Toby, 'but I can happily rephrase that as a no shit!'

'And if I hadn't suggested it?' asked Phillip playfully thinking, Thank Christ for your Liz having warned me about what could have been a severe career hiccup in my role as the *Pantastic* man.

'Simple,' laughed Toby, 'An invitation to meet for a drink, a tranquilizer *in* your drink followed by you waking up in the dentist's chair several hours later, smiling brightly!'

'Maybe I'll take you up on that!'

'Bollocks!' came the laughing reply, 'I'll get Liz to call you back.'

Phillip put down the phone. 'Fan-fucking-tastic *Pantastic*!' he laughed as he poured himself a glass of Stolichnaya with a dash of orange juice. '*Pantastic*, what an arsehole of a name but, if they see me as *their* Pan, the priapic half-man, half-goat Greek god of sex, well, who the fuck am I to argue!' Taking a long satisfying sip he continued with his musings. Great huh? The guy all guys fantasize over afraid of the fucking dentist! He gave a small, cynical chuckle. 'Talk about the most air brushed mouth in history,' he muttered, 'OK, let's go for it!'

Moving to his desk he checked his day-to-day diary. 'Dick Donald,' he murmured, 'Saturday 6.30, the restaurant bar, Claridges. Hmm, that's a first. Guy sounds quite kosher having suggested such a glamorous rendezvous. Interesting he wouldn't meet up here but then he has no idea who he's meeting and vice versa! Oh well, Claridges it'll be, new smile and all.'

Dick Donald's advert promoted on a popular gay channel showed an overweight, bald, middle-aged man smiling benignly, Buddha-like, at the camera. Unbeknown to his few work acquaintances and even fewer friends, the obscenely well-endowed, six foot three, much admired suave Phillip de Silva with his chiseled features, languorous emerald green eyes and dark wavy hair was an inveterate 'chubby chaser', his penchant being for very fat middle-aged men, preferably bald and a reminder of his Uncle Geoff who had willingly been seduced by Phillip, a precocious child of five. Phillip's lust for his uncle held no bounds, the devious little boy being insatiable in his perverse experimentations, these perversions, needless to say, being equally reciprocated.

'Phil, it's Liz. Friday ten o'clock with the Marquis de Sade!' Having given the address and a telephone number she continued. 'The session lasts about three hours which means you should be through around about one. Oh, hold on a sec.' There was momentary pause with voices heard talking in the background. 'Hi again, Toby says if you're up to it perhaps you would like to meet up at the Wolseley for an Evian water later?'

'*Evian water*? Why fucking Evian water?'

'Because we wouldn't want you staining your new gnashers while they're still fresh from their bleaching!' came Toby's jovial voice from somewhere close to Liz.

'Fuck off Tobe!' cried Phillip with a grin before putting down the phone.

FRIDAY:

A nervous Phillip arrived half an hour early for his appointment.

'Perfect! More time in which to attempt perfecting what already appears to be perfect!' said John Armstrong, an emaciated, silver-haired middle-aged man, his gleaming, slightly protruding eyeballs, pristine work jacket and sparkling teeth all whiter-than-white against his leathery sun-bronzed face. 'Follow me.'

The ghostly figure led Phillip briskly through to a large dimly lit room where the dentist's chair – Phillip's immediate thought on seeing the sleekly upholstered chrome monster being, Christ! A modern day version of something from the fucking Spanish Inquisition! – sat illuminated beneath a large arc lamp.

'This is Eva, my nurse,' said John Armstrong silkily. (Yeah, fucking Eva Braun, thought Phillip). 'If you'd like to hang your jacket over there we'll begin.'

Three hours later Phillip, his mouth still tingling, stepped out from the dental premises and hailed a passing taxi cab. 'Berkeley Square, please cabbie!' he said, giving the elderly cab driver a dazzling smile.

'You're that *Pantastic* bloke, ain't yer?' grinned the driver eyeing Phillip in the rear view mirror.

'I have to admit I am,' smiled Phillip, his smile even more dazzling.

'I'm one up on my missus then,' chuckled the driver.

'And why's that?' said Phillip still smiling but in his most gracious 'must be pleasant to the peasants' tone.

'She and Mavis – she's our youngest – always going on about what a looker you are but you never seem to smile.'

'Well, you certainly have one over them now, don't you?' chuckled Phillip and to prove his point stretched his lips even further, the double row of his now whiter-than-white perfection reflected dazzlingly in the driver's mirror.

Ringing the entry buzzer for the company situated on the floor beneath Toby's offices Phillip was able to take the lift up to the correct floor thus arriving unannounced outside the main door for Toby's company, *Aspirations Inc.* Without bothering to knock he bounced, smiling broadly, into the small reception area. 'Hi gorgeous!' he cried, his mouth blindingly white.

'Phil!' Liz shrieked. 'My God! Talk about a new you!' She shook her blonde head in wonderment, 'Do you know, in all the time I've known you – and it must be going on for four years – I have never, ever, seen you smile! My *God*,' she said again, 'You'll have every male worth his dick stampeding out to buy the new *Pantastic* toothpaste!'

'Is the boss in?' asked Phillip giving an even brighter – if possible – smile.

'He's on the phone but go on through and surprise him! If his reaction's anything like mine he'll be doubling your commission!'

Toby, a phone tucked under his chin and scribbling furiously on a note pad, gestured to his visitor to sit. Phillip did as bidden, sitting himself opposite the dapper man, his whiter-than-white smile frozen to his face. Christ, he thought, I'll be suffering from lockjaw if I keep this up but the reaction is certainly worth it. He grinned even more widely thinking, Hope to fuck this Dick Donald isn't expecting a blow job!

Glancing up at Phillip Toby simply let the phone drop from beneath his chin. 'Jesus fucking Christ, Phil! You look fucking *gorgeous*!'

Having spent the rest of Friday smiling dazzlingly at all and sundry an exhausted Phillip, his jaws aching, finally collapsed into bed but not before a final viewing of his whiter-than-white teeth in the former alien bathroom mirror. 'Christ, Phillip de Silva, even though I say it myself, you're one glorious bugger!'

The dazzling image still burning brightly in his mind the smug recipient – exhausted as he was – could not abstain from giving himself a languorous, glorious, Fountains of Tivoli-like wank.

SATURDAY:

Saturday evening being coolish saw Phillip wearing a stylish navy Gucci blazer, pale apricot shirt, charcoal-coloured trousers and the de rigueur Gucci loafers. Arriving at Claridges and having already smiled broadly at the cab driver, the doorman plus the reception staff, he made his way through the main sitting area adjacent to the exclusive Gordon Ramsay restaurant, a dazzling smile superimposed upon his artfully even more bronzed than usual face. Being immediately recognized Phillip stretched the already painful dazzling smile even further amidst the admiring whisperings ranging from

'Oh look, it's that Phillip de Silva, the man on TV, the *Pantastic* man' to 'Oh, isn't he to *die* for!'

Green eyes fixed determinedly on the entry leading to the small bar set to the right of the elegant Art Deco-styled eatery, he made his way confidently into the small luxurious venue. Glancing quickly at the occupants his gaze lighted on the solitary bulk of Dick Donald, the large bald head a perfect replica of the photograph in his advert, sitting silently in a corner, a plate of calorific nuts and cocktail nibbles placed alongside a champagne flute on the small, low black mirrored table in front of him. On seeing the dazzling *Pantastic* man making his way towards him, the vast, rotunda of a man gave a visibly large, wobbly start.

'Dick Donald, I do believe,' smiled Phillip even more whiter-than-whitely before adding in his most 'I'd like to suck you, fuck you and rim you' voice, 'Phillip de Silva, your date for the evening.'

'Jesus!' gasped the big man, his attempt at getting to his feet reminiscent of a defeated Sumo wrestler trying again to stand. 'Phillip de Silva, the *Pantastic* guy? I don't fucking believe it!'

'Apologies then, for it is and I am! But please, don't stand (the large figure immediately sank back down in a grateful heap) and, if I'm correct, your glass is almost empty so I trust you'll be joining me in another?' Phillip nodded towards the small space left on the banquette next to where Donald was once again sprawled. 'May I?'

'Err… yes, please do,' puffed the big man, 'that's if you think you'll have enough room,' he added with a glimmer of self-deprecating humour.

'Oh, I'm sure I can squeeze in, *Dick,*' said Phillip still smiling while giving his date a quick once-over, the fresh drinks having been quickly ordered. So like Uncle Geoff, it's bloody uncanny, he thought as, still smiling, he began to manoeuvre his way around the small table to the banquette. He's either got a massive one like Geoff's or else – as I've irritatingly found out before – it folds back into itself like a bloody putrid pink sea anemone! Whatever, I bet he's got a trunk full of toys to make up for fatso Dick's little dick! OK suit though, decent watch – Piaget I think – passable shoes. Obviously quite well heeled.

'So,' said Dick giving Phillip a nervous, blubbery smile. 'Do you do this often? I mean, arrange to meet guys like me?'

'No, not very often,' smiled Phillip, his face now appearing as if a severe case of rictus had settled in. 'But I can assure you one thing for certain, Dick' he added, attempting to combine an arch look along with his dazzling dentures, 'I can tell you here and now, having just met you, I'm very glad I did!'

'Oh,' said the big man in a surprisingly deep voice, 'Well, I don't need to begin our conversation by asking you your line of business, now do I?' His comment followed by a series of gigantic fleshy ripples.

'No, maybe not!' chortled Phillip, his jaw starting to seriously ache. 'And your line of business, Dick?'

'I'm an art restorer,' said Dick, 'I restore painting for a selection of galleries and auction houses.'

'Must be very interesting,' smiled Phillip gingerly reaching for his drink.

'Any hobbies, Phillip?' asked the man mound after a few moments of uncomfortable silence.

'I enjoy travelling,' came the smiling reply. 'So I suppose I'm lucky seeing my work finds me travelling a great deal to exotic and sometimes unheard of locations.'

'Yes, I saw those adverts you did for those dinner jackets. Taj Mahal, wasn't it?'

'Yes,' smiled Phillip imagining the giant man on all fours, Phillip trying to pull apart his immense, blubbery cheeks in an attempt to rim what would no doubt be a particularly hot, moist, malodorous cavity.

'Enjoy India?'

'Not particularly.' Phillip, still smiling, gave a small chuckle while moving his legs closer together in an attempt to disguise his growing hard-on at the thought of Dick's large arse writhing under the expertise machinations of Phillip's probing tongue. 'I'm not that keen on the smell of curry mixed with the smell of shit! I prefer to keep my olfactory pleasures separated!' the innuendo made with an almost superhuman stretching of his smile. 'And your hobbies, *Dick*?'

'I collect memorabilia,' said Dick, his large, moon-like face lighting up. 'I have quite a collection.' He gave a proud smile, his jowls descending in folds over his starched collar. 'I've even managed to get hold of the bowler hat Liza wore in *Cabaret.*'

'Oh really?' smiled Phillip thinking, No doubt there are *dozens* of gullible queens out there boasting about the same treasure.

'Would you like to see my collection?' suggested Dick, his small, currant-like eyes gleaming. 'I mean, we can have another drink here and then go round to my studio, it's quite close by. I have a small mews house off Marylebone High Street. We can then have a drink, you see my collection and afterwards I'd be honoured to take you out to dinner in my local.' He gave a wobbly laugh. 'Imagine the staff in my favourite when I walk in with Phillip de Silva!'

'Sounds great,' smiled Phillip, 'but why another drink here? Your mews house sound much more interesting.' By this stage Phillip was imagining Dick, still on all fours, whimpering in shuddering, globular-wobbling ecstasy as Phillip brutally fisted him, piston-like, right up to the elbow. Signaling to the barman he added, still smiling, 'These are on me.'

SEVERAL MONTHS LATER:

'This de Silva bloke's quite something, isn't he,' said Ted glancing up at Dick. He pointed to an open page in the glossy fashion magazine lying on his lap.

'Yeah,' said Dick pouring himself and Ted another large gin and tonic each. Handing the drink over to his young friend he added, 'Met him once. Arrogant bastard! Never stopped smiling! It was grin, grin, grin; just like some fucking Cheshire cat with George Clooney up its arse!'

'Nice smile, though,' observed Ted. 'Fabulous teeth.'

'False,' said Dick.

'No way,' laughed Ted. 'They're fucking brilliant!' He gave Dick a teasing grin. 'Rather like mine, don't you think?' he laughed, displaying a set off dull, yellowish molars.

'Nothing wrong with your teeth, Teddy love.' Dick nodded towards one of the many Victorian wood and glass display cabinets set around the small, claustrophobic, chintzy room. 'In there, next to the dried rose, the one Shirley Bassey threw me after one of her concerts.'

'What, the glass phial?'

'Yes. What's in there then?'

'Dunno,' muttered Ted, 'but I'll soon tell you.' Pulling himself to his feet he moved his thin, wiry frame over to the cabinet. Bending forward for a closer look he said disbelievingly, 'I thought at first they were white beads or something but it's full of fucking teeth!'

'Yes,' grinned Dick, 'Phillip de Silva's teeth.'

'Bollocks!' laughed Ted.

'No, teeth,' laughed Dick.

A FEW DAYS LATER:

'God forbid,' said Toby to Mavis in the privacy of his office as he countersigned the new contract with *Pantastic* for advertising their latest product, a new men's electric toothbrush *as used by Phillip de Silva.* 'God forbid they ever find out those aren't his teeth.' Toby gave a bitter laugh. 'And to think the stupid ponce was frightened of having his teeth *whitened*! Teach him to be more cautious about any future blind dates. GHB or some such shit in his drink, an address which doesn't seem to exist, a non-traceable phone number all added to which your so-called fucking date yanks out all your newly whitened fucking teeth with a pair of pliers? Bloody hell!'

'My thoughts exactly,' agreed Liz smiling down at the new contract lying on the desk in front of her employer. 'But don't let's knock it, Toby! Think of all that extra lovely money about to come rolling in!'

'Touché,' laughed Tony, 'What passes for a smile…'

'WELL FUCK ME SPORT!'

'It's quite bizarre,' said Jonathan to his guests. 'As you enter the club there's this set of screens with an assortment of glory holes, all at different heights. If you're in the mood for a blow job before or after the show, or both, all you do is stick your prick into one that suits and you'll be blown as never blown before!'

'You're joking?' said a flushed, obviously impressed Tony turning and looking excitedly at Malcolm, his equally flushed and excited companion. 'Hear that Malk? A blow job before *and* after the sex show!'

'Jeez, Tone,' said the red-faced Malk looking equally impressed.

'So, now or later or both?' laughed Jonathan in a patronizing tone as he observed the two inanely grinning English men in their badly tailored jackets, slacks and open neck shirts. Fucking tourists! he thought. Why must they make it so obvious that this is their first visit to the Far East and – even more apparent – their first visit to a sex show in no holds-barred-downtown Bangkok! Thank you for nothing, James Aldgate in giving these two morons my phone number!

'I think later,' said Tony giving Malk a sheepish look.

'Me too,' said Malk taking his lover by the hand.

Emboldened by the show during which the two young visitors were subjected to scenes of sexual deviations beyond their wildest imaginings and, noticeably fortified by several glasses of the house specialty, a lurid bright pink and extremely alcoholic drink, Tony and Malk, all former inhibitions forgotten, stood gently swaying and eyeing each other mischievously.

'I'm ready to try one of these screen blow jobs!' grinned Tony.

'Me too!' hiccupped Malk.

'Go ahead,' said Jonathan graciously. 'Ha ha! Please ignore the pun and forgive me if I don't join you. I'll be waiting in the bar.'

Within seconds Tony and Malk, their flies unzipped and pale erections pointing perkily joined the quirky line of men, a mix of young and old, some groaning and some gasping as they stood pressed against the front of the flimsy, shuddering wooden screens.

Side by side the two hastily selected their respective glory holes, quickly shoving their hard cocks through the dark apertures. Within seconds both were subjected to a hot, moist mouth and a sucking sensation as never experienced before.

'Well fuck me sport! A fuckin' blow factory! Fuckin' ace, mate!' bellowed a loud, raucous Australian voice followed by its owner, a puce-faced giant of a man who came staggering towards the gasping, grunting line.

'Fuckin' Christ!' he yelled stumbling drunkenly and losing his balance. 'Fucking shit!' he roared as he fell crashing – his massive arms outstretched – against the first of the screens causing the flimsy partition to collapse and taking along with it the neighbouring screen followed by the remainder.

The yells of indignation from the line of men were nothing in comparison to the high pitched screeches coming from beneath the collapsed wooden screens.

Tony and Malk, along with the rest of the put out – and pulled out – clientele watched horror-struck as various toothless old women who, seconds before had been sitting contentedly on their low stools behind the screens while placidly sucking away on the anonymous pricks, began to gradually emerge from under the wooden panels.

A PENCHANT FOR PENCILS

'Patrick will you *please* stop doing that!' Miss Barking, her rimless glasses with their thick lenses perched on the tip of her thin, pinched nose glared down at the scowling twelve year old sitting fidgeting behind his scarred school desk.

'Sorry Miss,' said Patrick slowly removing the offending article from his mouth but not before giving the pencil one last defiant chew before placing this – its end ragged and shiny wet – down in front of him.

'I'm surprised you've haven't worn your teeth down to the gums,' sniped the teacher, 'and I'm even more surprised you haven't given yourself *lead poisoning*!'

With a thin-lipped smile Miss Barking acknowledged the nervous tittering of the other pupils at her barbed witticism. A small, thin, grey-haired spinster, more sparrow-like than eagle, the elderly woman maintained an awesome reputation for her acidic put downs and her strong belief in '*Don't* spare the rod and *don't* spoil the child!'

The victim of the moment forgotten, Miss Barking returned to the front of the classroom where, daintily seating herself behind the teacher's table, she picked up the copy of Charles Dickens's *Bleak House* left lying there before the irritating confrontation with young Patrick.

'Now class, yesterday we reached page three hundred and sixty six, the end of chapter twenty two, which means today we begin chapter twenty three, headed *Esther's Narrative*. Please turn to the relevant page. Emily,' – she nodded towards the blonde, angelic-looking, twelve year old girl sitting a few desks away from Patrick – 'when you're ready, please start.'

Emily Archer – a smug expression on her face at having been chosen to start the lesson – began reading out loud in her high clear voice. After several minutes Patrick's mind – as with the minds belonging to the rest of the class – began to wander. Vaguely eyeing the elderly teacher who, although following the words in the book in front of her was also keeping a watchful eye on the class, her myopic grey eyes darting hither and thither amidst the supposedly reading pupils, the young boy couldn't resist a snigger. Silly old cunt, he said to himself, relishing the description picked up from Michael, his elder cousin, when discussing the teacher (Michael having sat in the same class a few years previously). What you need is a good old fuck, preferably by a donkey! (A regular suggested remedy put forward by Michael to alleviate the teacher's sour disposition). Aided and abetted by his cousin's lewd descriptions of a donkey wildly fucking an ecstatic Miss Barking, Patrick's mind was soon far removed from Emily's dissertation regarding the trials and tribulations of Dickens's heroine, the tiresome Esther.

'Thank you Emily,' said Miss Barking, her pinched mouth barely moving, 'That was good, very good. 'Patrick, will you please continue.'

Patrick looked up in blank astonishment having no idea as to which part of the chapter Emily had reached. 'Err... I can't, Miss,' said the young boy quietly before taking a deep breath before adding boldly, 'No, I can't!' Suddenly, feeling an extraordinary feeling of devilment surging through him, Patrick further added a further, 'and therefore I shan't!'

'Oh?' questioned Miss Barking, a thin, syrupy smile appearing on her bird-like face. 'And why *can't* you, Patrick? You seem to be forgetting that in *my* class there is no such word as *can't* and certainly no word such as *shan't*! Stand up!'

Rising slowly to his feet Patrick glared back at the smirking woman taking in her sallow complexion, her drab hair, drab clothes and all in all, her drab persona.

'Oh? And why *can't* you, Patrick?' said the boy, his voice a grotesque parody of the teacher's precise, high-pitched one. Giving a baleful laugh at the woman's startled expression Patrick found himself shouting in his boyish treble, 'Patrick can't, shan't and won't because you, Miss Barking, are a silly old cunt and what you need is a good old fuck, preferably by a donkey!'

A stunned silence descended upon the classroom, all the pupils looking at the evilly grinning boy in a combination of horror and exhilaration before slowly turning their eyes towards the teacher.

The tiny woman, her face white, her small bony hands clutching at her scrawny throat finally managed to speak. 'What did you just say?' she croaked, her voice barely audible.

Emboldened by the sniggers from Jack, his best friend and, surprisingly enough the precocious Emily, Patrick – to the breathless delight of the class – repeated loudly and enunciating every word as if speaking to a retard, 'I just said, Miss Barking, Patrick can't, shan't and won't because you, Miss Barking, are a silly old cunt and what you need is a good fuck, preferably by a donkey!' Suddenly, as if inspired he held aloft his chewed pencil. 'But maybe with this pencil for starters!'

Barely able to breathe the shocked woman – her wild, dilated eyes like large grey moons behind their lenses – staggered to her feet and with thin arms flailing, made a desperate attempt to reach the classroom door.

As the class watched her movements, more in fascination than alarm, Miss Barking managed a few more strangled gasps of 'help me, help me' before crumpling into a drab heap on the bare wooden floor.

Jack was the first to break the shocked silence. 'Is she dead?' he asked in his boyish tenor.

'I… err don't know,' said effeminate Gregory, the class's 'teacher's pet.' He looked triumphantly at a stunned Patrick. 'If she is you'll be tried for murder and jailed for life!' he smugly proclaimed.

'Hadn't we better call somebody?' said Emily, always practical.

'Yes, I'd better,' said Gregory making his way from his front row desk towards the door stepping gingerly over the small, huddled figure, a dark pool of urine growing on the floor around her. 'I'll go and get Mr. Bloom.' (Mr. Bloom being the headmaster).

'Oi!'

'Yes Patrick?' Gregory turned to look at the young boy, a supercilious expression having quickly replaced the smug one.

'If you say one word, just one word about me causing the old cunt to drop dead, you're next!' growled Patrick glaring unwaveringly at the boy, the former feeling of an inner power once again washing over him.

'Yes,' spoke up Jack. 'You'll definitely be next.'

'Can't you see, Gregory?' rang out Emily's high clear voice, an ally and friend. 'Patrick and his pencil have secret powers!'

'Beware,' chimed in Beth, Emily's best friend jumping at the chance of 'having a go' at the class's most disliked member.

'Yes, beware,' came another girlish voice.

'Beware! Beware!' chanted a few more as a white-faced Gregory, eyes wild, stumbled out through the doorway.

'Pooh, she doesn't half stink!' observed James, another class member.

'That's because when you die you shit and piss yourself,' piped up Emily knowledgeably.

As a result of Miss Barking's sudden demise, Langton (Private) Day School for Boys and Girls was closed for the next two days (Miss Barking having made her unforeseen departure on a Monday). Mr. Bloom, calling an emergency assemble to announce the decision, had taken the opportunity to remind the delighted pupils – their faces remaining suitably sombre for the occasion – what a tragedy it was to have lost such a devoted and much loved teacher. He had ended his speech balefully eyeing the assembled youngsters – several now openly grinning – by saying in his most sonorous voice, 'Miss Barking will be deeply missed.'

That evening Patrick, Jack, Beth and Emily met up at Emily's house where, acutely conscious of the shock Emily and her friends had been subjected to Mrs. Archer, Emily's anxious parent, being even more mother hen-like than usual as she bustled round the large rustic-styled kitchen plying 'the poor darlings' with sandwiches and endless glasses of orange juice.

After endless repetitions of 'Are you *sure* you dears are alright?' the woman finally left them alone so she could call Marjorie Monks, *her* best friend and discuss the excitement of the day.

'Do you really think she died because of what you called her?' giggled Emily.

'And something else,' said Patrick mysteriously, relishing his new role as the baddie of the morning's scenario.

'And what's that?' sniggered Jack, his freckled face wrinkling mischievously. Remembering his friend's wand-like waving of his pencil he couldn't resist adding, 'The power of the pencil?'

'Could be,' murmured Patrick giving his friends a narrow-eyed look. With an exaggerated shudder he added quietly, 'A pencil that has special powers.'

'Oh ho!' snorted Jack, flicking a hand through his unruly ginger hair. 'Do you hear that, Em and Beth? All of a sudden that chewed old bit of wood now holds hidden powers! Not only does it *taste* good but it also had the power to kill that silly old bitch!'

'Cunt,' said Emily, 'silly old cunt.' She held up a delicate hand staving off any comments before getting up from the table and tiptoeing theatrically over to the door. Listening for a moment, she then firmly shut the door before once again tiptoeing – much to the amusement of her three friends – over to the run of low cupboards containing the double sinks and draining boards. Quickly opening one she busily rummaged through an assortment of bottles before pulling out a bottle of Gordon's Gin. 'Dora the cleaner's secret bottle!' she whispered. No longer tiptoeing she scurried back to the table instead, deftly unscrewing the top and pouring a heft dollop into the four glasses. Within moments the bottle – topped up with water to its former level – was back in its hiding place and Emily back in her chair.

'That's *alcohol*!' breathed Jack, his green eyes wide.

'So?' said Emily loftily. 'Don't you ever read the papers? England has the biggest amount of underage drinkers in Europe!'

'I'll drink to that!' said Patrick with a grin.

'Me too,' giggled Jack.

'And me!' sniggered Beth.

'Tell you what,' said Patrick, the large dollop of gin having an immediate effect on his well-being and his innate new found powers. 'Just say this – my pencil power – does work, who should we do in next?'

'Gregory!' chorused Jack, Emily and Beth without hesitation.

'And after Gregory?' asked Jack, his brain now racing with a growing giddy excitement.

'My stupid mother,' said Emily firmly. 'She's another silly old cunt!'

'My elder brother,' said Beth. 'He's disgusting and always farting!'

'My dad,' said Jack quietly.

'Your dad?' questioned Patrick in a surprised voice.

'Yes, my dad,' whispered Jack.

'But why your dad?' asked Emily, picturing the large, ebullient Mr. Horner, chairman of a major City company, he and his wife two of the affluent area's most prestigious residents.

'Because he's a fucking poof!' snapped Jack, tears springing to his eyes.

'Your dad's *gay*?' cried Patrick, his eyes wide in disbelief.

'A queer?' whispered a shocked Beth.

'A homosexual?' said Emily, always one to have the last – and most erudite – word.

'Yes,' said Jack softly, 'and what makes it even worse my mum knows. She even knows his boyfriend! He's some poof decorator up in London.'

'A *boyfriend* up in London?' Emily, finding this revelation almost too much to handle made another quick dash to and from the sink cupboard.

'But surely it's the boyfriend who should die?' suggested Patrick, his mind beginning to swim alarmingly, 'and *then* your dad!'

'Maybe your right.' muttered Jack before adding a slurred, 'Absolutely! Boyfriend first and then Dad.'

'We must take an oath,' said the ever practical Emily.

'The oath of the pencils,' agreed Patrick, his speech thickening. 'But they must be *new* pencils!'

'New pencils,' slurred Beth.

'I have some in my pencil box,' said Emily, 'some are coloured but that makes it even more oath-like.' If anyone had any questions as to the young girl's grandiose comment they were not forthcoming. Reaching down for her satchel and nearly falling from her chair she uttered a loud 'shit!' before being grabbed hold of by a quick thinking Jack. 'Shit!' she said again as the contents from the satchel spilled with a clatter onto the ceramic floor. After several moments of a giggled scrabbling amongst her books, pens and other paraphernalia she finally came up with the pencil box. With more fumbling and giggles from all four Emily handed each of her friends a pristine pencil.

'First we must bite the ends three times then say "Power to the Pencils" before biting them a further three,' said Patrick making no attempt to disguise an unexpected hiccup. 'Afterwards, whenever you have a spare moment you must chew on your pencil and say once again, "Power to the Pencil."' Having listened solemnly to their friend's slow, carefully enunciated instructions the three friends solemnly bit into their pencils before quietly slurring the words 'Power to the Pencils' then biting the ends of their pencils once again.

'Poor dears,' Mrs. Archer (Mary Belle to her friends) sighed as she lay alongside Andrew, her stockbroker husband, later that night in their ornate, overly decorated four poster bed. The motherly woman, still tingling after her husband's unexpected demand for a fuck (it being a Monday night as opposed to the usual Saturday) gave another sigh. 'They must have been even more upset with Miss Barking's death than I had realized. Did I tell you Andrew I found the poor darlings sitting around the kitchen table almost *incoherent* in their grief and *chewing on pencils*?'

'Kids today,' murmured Andrew Archer while wondering why his wife was always such a dull fuck, only submitting to the missionary position and nothing else. What a contrast to Angie, his secretary. Now *there* was a fuck and a half! What a wildcat Angie was when they were at it on his office floor, doggie fashion or standing, sometimes bent over backwards against the edge of his desk and oh, those blow jobs! Talk about a fucking, sucking *industrial* hoover!

Desmond Horner sat looking at Richard, an incredulous expression on his handsome face. 'Please tell me you're not serious, Rikki? Please tell me you're not serious.'

'Oh, but I *am* Desmond, most serious,' replied the fey young man pushing aside a long, blond forelock with his thin, pale hand, a Cartier watch gleaming whitely on his slender wrist. 'It's either that or else young Richard here – *who isn't getting any younger, nota bene* – will have to think again.'

'But what you're asking is not only impossible but also hideously unfair!'

'What is? I certainly don't see asking you to divorce that irritating wife of yours and go through a civil ceremony with me as "hideously unfair." I see it as you being honest with yourself and honest with me.'

'But I thought we were happy as we are? And you know how fond Barbara is of you!'

'As we are?' Richard, his voice almost a shriek, his long thin hands fluttering as he reached for his Martini, gave his lover a glare with his carefully outlined eyes. 'Oh it's alright for *you*, Desmond,' he hissed, 'and benevolent bloody Barbara with your fabulous house and your glitterati party existence, but what about *me*? Always made to feel like the bit on the side. The convenient once or twice a week fuck! I love you, Desmond!' the young man added dramatically feeling he may just have overstepped the mark, 'I want to live with you, share your life.' With his big blue eyes widening even more he added in a tremulous tone, 'I want you to come home to *me*!'

'But…'

'No buts about it, Desmond,' said Richard, pursing his cupid bow lips. 'Alright, I know Barbara is most understanding about our relationship and I really appreciate how she has helped in promoting my business but enough is enough! Offer *her* enough, let her have that extravaganza of a house plus custody of that odious brat and I assure you'll she'll waft off quite happily into her multi-million pound future!'

'And if I don't?'

'You see *this*?' Richard pointed to his Martini glass. 'Watch.' With a flamboyant gesture the young man drained his drink. 'You see it now? Empty!' He tapped the arms of his comfortable armchair. 'You see this?' Standing up he pointed to the vacated seat. 'Empty!' He pointed to the doorway of the elegant cocktail bar where they had met for their usual evening rendezvous. 'You see that? It's the exit from this place. And you see this?' Here Richard pointed to his slim chest neatly encased in a smart Ralph Lauren jacket. 'This is now exiting through *that* exit!' Giving a haughty toss of his carefully contrived locks he added, 'When you've made your decision – *in my favour* – call me or else don't bother!' With that Richard, his shoulder bag in his hand, sashayed his way from the bar.

'Shit!' said Desmond, 'Shit!' he said again before beckoning over the smiling waitress and ordering another Martini.

'Whore! Bloody little whore,' he found himself muttering four Martinis later. 'You were *nothing* when I found you while working for that poncey designer brought in to redecorate our offices. Nothing until I became your lover and took you out of all that and setting you up in your own business.' Giving a brief snigger he gestured for another drink. 'Set you up in a nice little mews house as well; in fact, I've given you the bloody lot!' He shook his head in disbelief, 'And now you want *this*? Well young man, you can take a fucking running jump for starters! OK, it's been a great ride – literally – but there are plenty out there who would be more than happy with what you've got!'

Nodding a thank you for his fresh drink, Desmond continued muttering to himself. 'Pity you were so cavalier apropos any papers regarding the mews, young Richard. You'll be finding yourself homeless as from tomorrow, you ungrateful, silly little sod! As for the business? See how *that* crawls along once Barbara and her friends stop putting those rich, free spending clients your way. You silly, silly young man, don't you realize how fond Barbara really is of you? Why, it was my *wife* – so impressed when meeting you and seeing how you handled the design work to the offices –

who, even before we became lovers, suggested I set you up in your own business for Christ's sake!'

Making his way into Bond Street he hailed a passing taxi. Normally he would have driven back to the family home in Richmond but tonight he felt it 'better to be safe than sorry' thereby leaving the Jaguar in the office car park. While he could have telephoned his wife to say he would be staying over in the small flat housed on the top floor of his Berkeley Square offices, this particular evening the distraught man was desperate to get home to his family.

'Good evening dear.' Walking over to his wife sitting curled up on a sofa in the comfortable study, a book on her lap, he lent down giving the elegant blonde woman a kiss on her cheek.

'You're late, darling,' smiled Barbara adding, 'Oh dear, I know that face. *Not* a good day and correct me if I'm wrong, several over-comforting Martinis?'

'Day OK, evening not so OK, hence the Martinis.'

'Let me guess, young Rikki playing up again?'

'Spot on.' Desmond pointed to the drinks cupboard, 'Care to join me?'

'I was having a glass of wine but if you're still in a Martini mood I wouldn't say no. I take it you didn't drive back?'

'No way, José! Ever since Bob was breathalysed last month one daren't take the risk.' Desmond moved over to the drinks cupboard where he began preparing a pitcher for the two.

'So what now with the monster child?'

Desmond gave a dry laugh. 'Which one? Ours or Richard.'

'In a way both,' laughed Barbara. 'Maybe I should be rueing the day I suggested you back the little genius in his own business.' She gave another small laugh. 'Talk about shooting oneself in the foot!'

Handing her a brimming Martini glass Desmond sat down in his favourite chair opposite her. 'It should have, could have worked, you being so understanding about it all; me being bisexual, adoring and still adoring you but never being able to let that other side of me go.'

'I did what I did and do what I do because I love you Desmond and that's all there is to it. You and Jacko are my life and no matter what shenanigan's you get up to you know you'll always be forgiven.' Barbara gave her husband a penetrating look. 'Now what's he done?'

'Wants me to divorce you and go through a civil ceremony with him!'

'And?'

'I told him to take a running jump!' Desmond gave a tired sigh. 'I'll have the locks changed to the mews and get Andy to have all his furniture collected and put in store or else delivered to an address that young idiot can give him. (Andy being the company's elderly caretaker, gay and totally devoted to Desmond and Barbara).

'Are you sure about this?'

Putting down his glass Desmond lent across the butler's tray table and took hold of his wife's hand. 'Babs, when push comes to shove, you and Jacko take priority, *not* my gay bit on the side.' He suddenly looked at his wife, his handsome face deeply concerned. 'You don't think Jacko has any inkling about all this, do you? Our understanding? My set up?'

'I doubt it, darling. After all, Jacko's only twelve and far more interested in computer games or spending whatever spare time he has with that precocious Patrick Prendergast and twelve-going-on-for-twenty Emily Archer!'

'Good. Because I love our Jacko to bits and wouldn't do anything to hurt him.' Desmond took another long sip of his Martini. 'Christ! Imagine the poor lad ever having to cope with a father who's a closet gay. I can remember being around his age and coping with being twelve going on thirteen was quite enough, the gay thing making itself known later.'

Jack, intrigued by the late arrival of a taxi outside the house, his curiosity strengthened by his father's cautious walk from the cab to the house, had slipped silently down the stairs where he had positioned himself outside the study door. Minutes later the ashen-faced boy returned to his room, his head spinning. 'Dad loves me, he really loves me and Mum,' he kept saying to himself, 'our happiness means more to him than his own.' Picking up the newly bitten pencil from where he had placed in prime position alongside a piece of brightly painted concrete, a souvenir remnant of the Berlin Wall, he raised it to the open window. 'Power to the Pencils' he whispered, 'Power to the Pencils.'

'So,' said Patrick looking at Jack and Emily, Beth having been unable to join them, 'it's time to begin our campaign.'

This particular Saturday morning, five days after the demise of Miss Barking, saw the three seated comfortably in the den of the Patrick's parents' house, a large red brick Victorian edifice set in a manicured garden of half an acre, Gill Prendergast's (Patrick's mother) pride and joy.

'Yes,' agreed Emily in her usual brisk manner before giving the two boys a sheepish look. 'I'm sorry,' she whispered, 'but I can't quite remember what we said. I remember taking an oath and chewing on our pencils…' – to prove her point she quickly produced her chewed pencil from her small tote bag – 'but apart from that it's all a bit of a blur.'

'Me neither,' said Jack nodding solemnly. He added in a sonorous voice, 'It was that gin and now we're all alcoholics because alkies suffer severe memory loss!'

'Well *I* remember,' said Patrick smugly. 'We planned to kill Gregory, Emily's mum and your dad, Jacko, because he's gay. We also planned to kill his boyfriend!'

'We did?' said Emily, giving Jack an anxious glance.

'We did and you called your mother an old cunt!' said Patrick with a smirk. 'And you, Jacko, called your dad a fucking poof!'

'I did?'

'Yes you did. What's more you almost started to blub when you were telling us!'

'Oh,' said Jack looking shamefacedly down at his feet, his mind darting back to the domestic scene between his parents the night before.

'I think I must have been drunk,' announced Emily looking immensely pleased with herself. 'Yes,' she said, nodding her head emphatically, 'which makes me yet another of those underage drinkers.'

'Me too,' said Jack giving Emily an encouraging smile. 'Therefore we can't be held responsible for our actions!' he added loftily.

'Fine allies you're turning out to be,' sulked Patrick, 'even though you took an oath!'

'It wasn't really an oath oath,' insisted Jack. 'We didn't mix drops of blood, shake hands even or do any of the things you're meant to do when taking or making an oath.' He looked down at his shoes once more. 'Besides, things have changed. I really don't wish to kill my dad even though I wouldn't say no to his boyfriend.'

'And I really don't really want to kill my mum,' said Emily.

'And I suppose Beth feels the same way about her farting older brother? Huh!' Patrick gave the two a glare. 'Some friends you've turned out to be! So, I'm alone am I? The only Pencil Power left?'

'It's all because of the alcohol,' said Emily in her most firm voice. 'And like Jack, I can't be held responsible for my actions.'

'OK then,' said Patrick resignedly. 'Anyone want a Coke?'

Sunday afternoon saw Patrick and Jack meeting up at Jack's parents' house where, after a swim in the indoor pool, the two boys sat, de rigueur Coca Cola in their hands, watching a DVD of Spiderman 2.

'I'm curious,' said Patrick, 'Why the change of heart about killing your dad.'

'Because I got it all wrong!' blurted out an anguished-looking Jack, the young boy almost sick with remorse. 'My dad loves me and mum – I heard him telling her so Pat – and is never going to see the boyfriend again!'

'So he's no longer gay?'

'I don't think so.'

'And he's come back to you and your mum?'

'Yes.'

'Good. But what about the boyfriend? He could have done a lot of damage.'

'I know.' Jack took a deep breath before telling his best friend all. 'He wanted dad to divorce mum and *marry* him like that Elton John and his boyfriend did!'

'And your dad said no?'

'Told him to take a running jump!'

'So the Power of the Pencils could still kill the boyfriend?'

'If you really must.'

'And Gregory?'

'Maybe, maybe not.'

'But the boyfriend a definite yes?'

Jack let out a long sigh. 'Well, it would teach him a lesson.'

'Hmm,' said Patrick taking another sip of his Coke, the actions of *Spiderman* totally forgotten. 'We'll really have to put on our thinking caps Jacko. I've never killed anyone before.'

'Nor me.'

'Shall we talk to Em? After all, she's quite clever for a girl.'

'Why not?'

A hysterical Richard had made a dramatic appearance at *The Grove*, the Horner's elegant Georgian-styled house the day after his threat to leave Desmond had so devastatingly backfired. Having been met at the front door by a tight lipped Barbara and Tim Fortescue, the family lawyer (Desmond being away in Munich on business for the next two days) he was told in no uncertain terms to leave before the police were called. To the young man's chagrin, Barbara – having anticipated such a reaction following an threatening phone call from the young man earlier – had summonsed Tim Fortescue not only to be present from an professional point of view but also for dinner, Tim being Barbara's lover. Jack, who had been doing his homework in his bed room had sneaked out onto the upstairs landing where he had witnessed, wide-eyed, the dismissal of the wretched Richard.

'*Richard Bingham*?' said Emily incredulously. 'Why, Marjorie Monks, mummy's best friend just commissioned him to redo their house!'

'See,' said Patrick, 'already the Power of the Pencils is beginning to show!'

'So what do we do?' asked Jack, now back to his old self seeing he was no longer under an obligation to kill his father.

'This is what we do,' said Patrick.

'You *can't* do that!' said Emily a few minutes later, her face filled with genuine horror as the enormity of Patrick's suggestion hit home.

'No way,' said Jack, his expression a replica of Emily's.

'Oh can't I?' said Patrick eyeing his two companions with disdain. 'Maybe *you* can't but I certainly can!' He gave a snort. 'Obviously the "Power to the *Pencils*" is now the singular "Power of the Pencil!"'

'Don't do it Patrick,' said Jack softly to his friend. 'If you do, you'll never hear from me again.'

'Nor me,' said Emily firmly.

'See if I care,' said Patrick as he got up and left the two sitting silently in the Archer's den.

SEVEN YEARS LATER:

An anxious Patrick looked down at his watch his mind flashing back to his class earlier that day where he and another student had been asked to recite Lewis Carroll's complicated *The Lobster Quadrille*. 'Oh Mr. Horner,' he muttered, a small smile playing on his lips, 'Are you really the "enlightening to my tail?"' Giving a giggle he took a sip from his drink before asking himself coquettishly, 'Will you, won't you, will you want romance?'

'Patrick!' said the cheerful voice, 'You found the place! Sorry to be late but bloody Tobias Black, our US associate got utterly pissed at lunch and then we couldn't get rid of the old sod!'

'Some lunch,' said Patrick his voice lightly chiding, 'to last until eight!'

'Well,' snorted Desmond, 'you know Americans! Mr. Black insisted, but simply insisted we all go back to the Dorchester for even more drinks.' He gave the young man a beaming smile. 'Well I must say Mr. Prendergast, for someone who had so little sleep last night you're looking remarkably spry!' He lent forward giving Patrick's knee a gentle squeeze. 'Lovely to see you again and thank you for waiting.' The big man sat back on the banquette. 'However enough is enough so after a token glass I made my excuses explaining my wife had a dinner party organized.'

'I do?' camped Patrick.

'Hopefully with me,' laughed the big man. 'Ah, Antonio.' He smiled up at the hovering waiter before turning back to Patrick and pointing at his Martini glass. 'Vodka or gin?'

'Vodka.'

'I'll have the same please, Antonio and I'm sure Mr. Patrick won't say no to another.'

'It would be a first if I did!' said Patrick archly.

Seven years after the dissolution of the short-lived Power to the Pencils club, Patrick, now a strikingly handsome, languid eighteen year old and a student at famous Royal Academy of Dramatic Art – or RADA to give it its every day name – found himself invited by Jeremy, his closest gay friend to a private party in elegant Chelsea which 'Jer' promised would be a laugh, if nothing else.

Patrick having 'come out' while at senior school, his latent gayness being given the go ahead – almost literally – by an unexpected lusting for Bobby Brewer, the head boy, which to Patrick's delight had proved to be mutual. Once initiated into the delights of gay sex by the aforesaid Bobby and finding himself involved in a whole new world, Patrick soon latched onto Jeremy after meeting the stylish young man at one of the endless gay parties he now frequented. The fact that he and Jeremy were attending the same drama school proved an added bonus.

'The party's being given by some grand old queen, some writer who apparently writes gay porn. A Robert... Robin... Ronald Anderson or someone like that. Ever heard of him?'

'Oh yes, one or two of his books have been made into films. One, *The Gallery* even made old Freddy on Elm Street look tame!'

'That's the guy. Anyway, he's giving this bash at his place in Chelsea so why not come along? Lots of booze, fabulous food and lots of available c-o-c-k or so I'm told.'

'C-o-c-k? Am I to take it you mean an orgy of wild abandoned sex?'

'Hardly! I think you'll find the majority of guests a lot of prissy old and not so old queens.' Jeremy gave a mischievous laugh. 'When I said fabulous food and lots of available c-o-c-k I was referring to the waiters. They're all from that gay catering company where all the staff are David Beckham and Jude Law lookalikes!'

'Count me in!' laughed Patrick, 'or, knowing my tastes, count them *in*!'

The venue, held in a grand duplex flat overlooking the Chelsea Embankment, proved to be as Jeremy had anticipated, a group of well-heeled middle-aged to elderly gays along with a scattering of young men, some obviously gay and some extremely butch-looking. 'Quite a little gathering of escorts in our midst,' hissed Jeremy reaching for two champagne flutes from a handsome passing waiter. 'See that big number over there? Advertises in QX magazine. Boasts a ten inch cock! And that screamer over there, she's that television host show who, I should think, boasts *no* cock to shriek of! But the waiters! Talk about Sodom and Grrrrrr!'

After a brief introduction to their dapper host and his smiling instructions to 'enjoy yourselves,' Patrick found himself momentarily standing alone while Jeremy chatted busily to minor film director.

'Patrick? Patrick Prendergast?' said a friendly but hesitant voice alongside him.

Looking round the young man found himself facing Desmond Horner, Jack's father, a bemused expression on the big man's handsome face.

'*Mr.* Horner!' exclaimed Patrick, rapidly thinking back, But of course, Jack's gay father and the problematic bitchy boyfriend who'd experienced – thanks to Patrick – a most unexpected and hideous attack all those years ago. Well, well, well but then, why should I be surprised to see you at a gay gathering, Mr. H? After all, old habits never die!

'Mr. Horner? Desmond, please,' laughed the genial man. 'I appreciate I'm Jacko's father but I'm not *that* decrepit! Well, not yet!' He gave another friendly chuckle while giving Patrick an appraising once over.

'I must say Patrick – as I always said to Babs, Jacko's mother – that Prendergast boy is going to grow into a stunner and cause of a lot of broken hearts, both male and female!'

'You did?' laughed a delighted Patrick.

'We both did,' smiled Desmond. 'Ah,' reaching for two flutes of champagne from a Jude Law lookalike he handed one over to Patrick which saw the young man now holding two, a bemused smile playing on his face.

'Curiously enough Jacko mentioned you the other evening. Apparently you didn't see each other after you went on to your separate senior schools, so perhaps you didn't know he skipped university preferring to join our company as a novice in the Hong Kong office. I must say he's done us proud!' Desmond took a sip of his drink. 'His exact words were, in fact, "I wonder what happened to Patrick? Now there was a Bosie in the making!"'

'Bosie?'

'As in Oscar Wilde's Bosie,' laughed Desmond.

'Oh?' Patrick gave out a light laugh. 'For a moment I thought you said *boozy*!' He gave another laugh. 'I don't know why I'm even remembering this or, more to the point, even whether I should be telling you but thinking you said boozy reminds me of a silly oath, vow whatever, Jacko, Emily and Beth – that's right, little Beth Carter – made some six or even years ago having gotten completely pissed on your cleaner's hidden stash of gin in our orange juices!'

'Oh, gin at the tender age of twelve or thirteen was it?' Desmond gave a laugh. 'And here I was in two minds about offering you that other glass of champagne!'

'Yes, we snuck a drop or two from Dora, the daily's hidden bottle!'

'And got pissed and made an oath?'

'Yes,' said Patrick feeling slightly ridiculous and beginning to regret he'd mentioned the incident.

'May I ask what this gin inspired oath involved?

'Well, if you must know it involved something nasty happening to you, Emily's mother, Beth's brother and the school sneak, a nasty little shit called Gregory.'

'Oh, and who was to be your intended victim or whatever?'

'Ah,' said Patrick, uncomfortable by Desmond Horner's endless questions said with a mysterious smile, 'I'd already dealt with my evil deed.'

'Dare I ask what the oath involved?'

'Oh, nothing worse than an attack of acute diarrhea, preferably in a very crowded and very public place. Nothing serious but when you're twelve or so, shitting yourself in public would have been mega!'

'Yes, an attack of the shits in the middle of Harrods could have been quite an embarrassment!' laughed Desmond, beaming broadly at the young man. 'Now I come to think of it, Jacko also mentioned something about this when we were discussing you.'

Jeremy seeing his friend getting on so well with perhaps the best looking – and most affluent-looking – man in the crowded room had left the two talking before quietly slipping away and giving one of the David Beckham lookalikes a blow job to be remembered. On returning to the party he discovered Patrick and Desmond had left together a few minutes earlier.

Next day as they sat outside eating their usual sandwiches and sharing a bottle of mineral water a mischievous Jeremy, barely unable to contain himself had blurted out, 'How was it?'

'How was what?' asked Patrick, equally as mischievously.

'Your night with granddad Midas?'

'Fucking fabulous!' opined Patrick.

'Where did you err... end up?'

'Back in Desmond's office. He has a self-contained suite there for when he works late or has been entertaining clients.'

'Ah ha! In other words a fuck pad!'

'If you insist!'

'I do!' Jeremy gave another giggle. 'Is he, is it...?'

Patrick picked up the plastic water bottle. 'Christ no!' he laughed on seeing Jeremy's expression. 'No, more Coke bottle which, let's face it, is pretty substantial!'

'You lucky bastard!' breathed Jeremy.

'And plucky!' grinned Patrick. 'And I can assure you when I say Coke bottle I mean the real McCoy!'

'Jesus,' said Jeremy bursting into a fit of the giggles. 'If push came to show I would even be able to handle a *Dieted* Coke bottle!'

'Cunt!' laughed Patrick giving his friend a friendly punch on the shoulder.

'Better a cunt than a gigantic, over stretched arsehole!' yelped Jeremy dodging another punch.

'And further more!' adding Patrick, laughing even more, 'We're meeting again this evening!'

It was Desmond's turn to look at his watch. 'Good heavens! Is that the time? Where would you like to go for dinner? How does Scalini sound to you?' Scalini being a top Chelsea Italian eatery in exclusive Walton Street.

'Scalini's sounds great.' Patrick gave an impish grin. 'And after Scalini's?'

'Sadly I do have to be home. It's Jacko's last day with us tomorrow – he and Babs were dining with friends locally – but how about the following evening.' Desmond gave a sheepish smile. 'There's someone I'd like you to meet, someone I couldn't help bragging to about you! Tell you what, why don't I collect you from RADA; we can get a few bottles of wine and order a pizza when we get to Leo's.'

'Leo?'

'An old friend, an antiques dealer and restorer along with being a collector of the bizarre. Leo lives with his partner Vulcan – no, I joke not – in a rather weird and wonderful converted church in Wapping. His home is certainly worth seeing. Very Tim Burtonish, if there's such a word or term.' Desmond gave out a small laugh. 'He has two massive plate glass topped coffee tables, his coffin tables he calls them, their bases being actual bona fide coffins.'

'I can't wait,' laughed Patrick, 'like I can't wait for that pasta!'

'So be it, pasta tonight with pizza night after next.'

'Sounds good to me and after pizza night after next?'

'I think I may very well be working late and stay over at the office, something requiring my undivided attention!'

Dinner concluded Patrick waved a farewell as Desmond drove off along the quiet Chelsea Street, the young man having refused a lift back to his flat in Markham Square saying, 'It's only a short walk and after all that delicious pasta the walk will do me good.'

Cutting down Draycott Avenue he made his way into Tryon Street passing a well-known gay pub, The Queen's Head. 'Just in time for a nightcap,' he muttered eyeing the warm glow emanating from the pub's windows. 'One and one only and then home to beddy-byes!'

Inside the busy pub Patrick quickly ordered a large vodka tonic before standing against a nearby column while surveying the animated gay drinkers while thinking, silly queens, instead of standing around here shrieking and squeaking you should be out and about finding yourself someone worthwhile! He gave a slight snigger, Jesus Jacko, now there's a turnabout, me ending up with your old man. Giving another snigger he couldn't help muttering, 'Should we ever meet what would Desmond introduce me as? Your new step *mum*?'

'Pardon?' said a startled voice. 'Did you just call me mum?'

Patrick glanced up to see a plump, ruddy-faced middle-aged queen looking at him, a facetious smile on his jowly face. 'No,' said Patrick sharply, 'I didn't call you mum, in fact I wouldn't want to call you *anything* so fuck off, fatso!'

'Well excuse me!' gasped the fat queen before waddling off amongst the other drinkers.

Back in his small flat Patrick removed his jacket and kicked off his loafers before putting on a CD (Michael Bublé) and pouring himself another drink. Making himself comfortable on the sofa he sat thinking about his chance meeting with Desmond plus the fact that Desmond just happened to be the father of his best childhood friend. Once again Desmond had brought up the young people's initiation into the unpleasant aftermath of a hangover. 'Obviously Jacko never filled you in on the whole story – *my* part that is – never told you the rest,' mumbled Patrick gazing blankly towards the open window. 'And just as well you'll never ever fucking know.'

An impatient Patrick stood waiting for Desmond outside the Academy's theatre in Gower Street. 'Jesus, seven fucking fifteen,' he muttered glancing at his watch. 'If you say six thirty make it six thirty! I'll give you another five minutes and that's it. There are a lot of cocks out there for the taking.' Giving a snort at his innuendo he then continued. 'I could have joined Jer and co in the pub rather standing round like some lovelorn wally.' He gave his watch another furtive glance. 'Right, that's it. I'm off.'

A loud hooting stopped in his tracks as Desmond drew to a screeching halt alongside the walking figure. 'Sorry Patrick,' came the apologetic voice. 'But the traffic to here was hellish!'

'Desmond!' cried Patrick going into his best carefree RADA inspired mode. 'What are a few more minutes when one knows they're worth waiting for!'

'I bet you say that to all your paramours!' laughed Desmond giving Patrick's thin knee a gentle squeeze. 'In there,' he said, nodding towards the glove compartment, 'a small anniversary present.'

'Anniversary?'

'Well Patrick, it *is* the third day since we met properly so why not a small celebratory gift?'

'But it's a Cartier watch!' exclaimed Patrick looking at the famous white rectangular face with the black numerals.'

'Just to make sure you have no excuse for being late when we've arranged to meet,' said Desmond with a mischievous chuckle.

Half an hour later they swept past the Tower of London and after a few more minutes turned into Wapping High Street with its cobbled streets and picturesque warehouses now converted into luxurious homes. 'Leo's church-cum-studio-cum-home,' said Desmond drawing to a halt outside a Victorian grey stone church.

'He actually owns this?' said Patrick looking up at the gloomy edifice silhouetted against the evening sky. 'But it's massive!'

'Wait until you see inside,' laughed Desmond reaching into the back of the car for a carry bag containing several bottles of wine. 'It's fairly mind blowing!' he added while inserting a key with his free hand into the lock of the massive oak door, the key attached to his own key ring.

Leo turned out to be a sprightly seventy years old. 'He's exactly like Disney's Geppetto, the old wood carver in *Pinnochio*!' whispered Patrick as they followed the elderly man into the vault-like building.

'This is amazing,' said Patrick looking around the main body of the church with its series of cantilevered platforms housing what Leo described as 'living quarters and more!'

'As you can see,' explained Leo with a sweeping gesture, 'It's a mixture of Bauhaus, bric-a-brac and whatever takes our fancy!' He pointed to a long, wide old work bench. 'Over there for example, screwed to or displayed on that old oak bench you've got everything that works at the turn of a screw or when being turned or screwed. These range from old fashioned mincing machines, a working lathe, a selection of vices, a wind-up gramophone, pencil sharpeners, meat grinders, vegetable slicer, potato cutter, wind up mechanical dolls, even a wind-up windmill – you name it, it's there! I call that display my little tribute to Henry James.'

'Henry James?' questioned a completely bewildered Patrick taking the heavy pewter goblet of wine proffered by the animated little man.

'Yes, Henry James and his *Turn of the Screw*. Everything on the table turns or screws!' Leo gave a snigger. 'Would you believe it, even *I've* been screwed on that very same bench! Oh yes, numerous times in those blissful, hedonistic days of yore!'

Mad, bloody fucking barking mad, thought Patrick eyeing the grinning little man warily over the rim of his goblet. 'And that?' he asked pointing to a long low wooden edifice. 'Don't tell me...'

'Good old fashioned stocks and yes, I've been locked into those as well for a delicious evening of S and M!'

'As one does, or is,' muttered Patrick giving Desmond a nervous glance. To his alarm Desmond seemed to be immersed in a copy of the Evening Standard lying open on a nearby console table made out of antlers.

'I like the sketches,' said Patrick taking another sip of his drink and swallowing nervously. 'Very architectural.'

'Ah yes, they're scenes of Wapping High Street and other local byways. Those you're admiring are pen and ink, over here are some pencil sketches, portraits mainly and one or two charcoal drawings, again of our neighbourhood.'

'And the artist?'

'My partner Vulcan who should be joining us any minute from now. Like our other guest with the pizzas!' Leo turned and called across to Desmond. 'Jay said he's collect the pizzas on his way.'

'He did? Oh good,' replied Desmond non-committedly.

'Another drink Patrick?' asked Leo adding, 'and of course you must take a proper look at the coffee tables!'

'Ah yes,' said Patrick snidely, 'the famous *coffin* tables. Very droll or even macabre if I may say so, but then rather in keeping with living in a church!' He gave a small laugh. 'All mod cons should one suddenly drop dead in the middle of dinner!'

'Precisely,' said Leo with a grin. 'Ah, saved by the bell and please note Patrick, when I say bell that *is* the original church bell you're hearing which is activated when one presses the bell at the front door.'

'I'll get it!' called a voice.

Old friend or not, once those fucking pizzas are finished, I'm out of here, said Patrick to himself, Desmond or no Desmond. This place is like the fucking Munsters!

'Pizzas, Jay and *moi*! what more could you ask for?' said Vulcan walking into the room followed by a grinning Jack holding three large boxes of pizzas.

'Remember Jay – or Jacko as you used to call him? Delayed his return to HK so as to be here this evening,' smiled Leo. 'And of course you won't recognize Vulcan but you two have met before. Quite by *accident* if my sources are correct.'

Patrick stared first at Jacko who seemed a duplicate of his father and then at the hideously scarred, hairless second man, his face a twisted mess of burned skin, his mouth a small crooked hole and a few twisted whorls of flesh where his ears should have been. But it was his eyes which terrified Patrick, a pair of the palest blue he had ever seen and filled with an unbelievable hatred.

The terrifying apparition held out a perfectly formed hand. 'I've been so looking forward to meeting you again,' said the destroyed face in a soft croaking sound. 'Leo affectionately calls me Vulcan, after the Greek god of fire, but we've met once before, seven years ago today, when I was Richard Bingham.' The distorted face turned towards a grim-faced Desmond who meanwhile had quietly moved forward and closer to Patrick. 'You did give him the anniversary present, I trust?'

Desmond gave a small nod.

'Good, thank you Desmond,' came the croaked reply. Turning again to a stunned Patrick the scarred persona of Richard Bingham, former interior decorator, said softly, 'Well, what are we waiting for?'

'Noooo!' screamed Patrick rushing forward in an attempt to reach the front door.

'No you don't!' shouted Desmond making a grab for the panic-stricken figure. 'Grab him Jay!' he yelled to his son as Patrick slipped from his grip. Within seconds the thickset young man had grappled Patrick to the ground where he was immediately joined by his father and Leo in holding the struggling young man down while Richard deftly handcuffed him.

Lifting Patrick roughly to his feet Desmond flung him contemptuously into a nearby chair. 'Shut up!' he yelled as Patrick began to scream. 'Shut up!' he yelled again before giving the young man a hefty slap across the face. 'One more sound out of you,' Desmond hissed, 'and I'll fucking gag you!'

'What are you going to do to me?' whispered a sobbing Patrick not daring to raise his voice. He looked up at Jack and his father imploringly. 'I thought we were friends, lovers?' he added hoarsely.

'Vulcan, Rikki is my lover,' hissed Desmond, 'and will always be while you, you poisonous little piece of shit are *nothing*!'

'But... but...' burbled Patrick.

'Did you really think I'd do anything to hurt Dad?' snorted Jack. 'Just because your family life is a complete fuck up, don't think everyone else's is!' He took hold of Richard's hand. 'I've come to know and love Rikki like the brother I never had. OK, he caused a bit of a problem but it could have been easily resolved. In fact it *had* been resolved and then you had to "go it alone" and fuck everything up!'

Jack gave Richard's hand an affectionate squeeze. 'I'll go to my grave regretting that I never took you and your threat seriously, you vile walking virus,' he snarled at Patrick, 'but now it's your turn. Time to put him in the stocks, don't you think Dad? Leo? Rikki!'

As threatened Desmond, using a torn strip from a convenient piece of batik patterned fabric draped over the base of a nearby statuette, quickly gagged the hysterically screaming Patrick. Despite his almost sub-human struggles the young man – handcuffs removed – was firmly locked in the stocks, his gagged head swinging wildly from inside the clamped opening, his forearms sticking out on either side.

'Remember your "Power to the Pencils" Patrick?' said Desmond. 'Why not "Power to the Blow Torch"? After all, that's what you used on Rikki's face when you sneaked into the Monks's house that morning where – thanks to the unthinking Emily – you'd been told he'd be there by himself taking photographs and making some sketches before meeting Marjorie Monks and Mrs. Archer locally for lunch.' The big man lent down, his tearful face close to the wide-eyed Patrick. 'You took a small, portable butane blow torch to my lover's *face*; the love of my life, the man I still love and will love forever *with* both my son and my wife's blessing!'

Patrick could only offer a strangulated moan while looking beseechingly at Jack.

'No use looking at me, Patrick,' said Jack coldly. 'I told you that day that Dad loved me and Mum and once I knew that, all your ridiculous threats and ploys meant nothing! Nothing at all! The police couldn't prove anything; an unwarranted attack, the masked intruder never traced! But I knew, we *all* knew!' He looked at Richard staring transfixed by the struggling figure in the stocks. 'Rikki? You ready to do the honours?'

'Oh yes,' croaked Richard.

'Leo?'

'Phase one ready,' said Leo handing over the manual commercial pencil sharpener to Desmond for him to grip as Richard moved forward and grabbed Patrick's writhing left hand.

Without hesitation Richard took hold of Patrick's little finger and, squeezing it into the aperture of the pencil sharpener, slowly began to turn the handle as Desmond, Jack and Leo began to softly chant, 'Power to the Pencil, Power to the Pencil.'

It took only three fingers before Patrick passed out.

Patrick never returned to RADA. Several weeks later a curious Jeremy contacted his parents to see when he would be returning to the school. It was only then that Patrick was reported missing.

THREE YEARS LATER:

'Here's to the third anniversary of "Power to the Pencil"' laughed Desmond raising his glass in a toast.

'To the Power of the Pencil!"' chorused the four men sitting around the table in Desmond and Richard's home.

'To you, my darling, forever,' said Desmond smiling gently at the scarred Richard and getting a soft wave in return. 'And to you, dear Leo for coming to look after us, my dear Rikki and me, when we moved in our very special home here those traumatic ten years ago. To Leo, dear Leo, our very old, much loved Queen Friday!' He gave another smile. 'And last but not least a toast to Jacko and Chan, my son and son-in-law over here from China especially for today anniversary celebration.'

'Stop being such a sentimental old queen, Dad!' laughed Jack. 'Having seen how happy you've always been with Rikki why would I want to be anything else *but* gay!' The handsome young man gave a happy laugh before blowing a kiss at the smiling young Chinaman. 'And don't let's forget Mum, she's been an absolute brick!' Jack lifted his glass. 'To Mum and Anthony, her new husband. May they be as happy as we all are tonight.'

'Need any help with the washing up, Leo?' asked Desmond later.

'No, no dear man, it's all in the dishwasher. All I have to do is turn it on!' He gave Desmond a sly glance before adding with a chuckle. 'Not like that night three years ago! Christ, remember the effort and the mess!'

'Would I ever!' Desmond gave a companionable laugh. 'We must have been mad.'

'We were, but also madly in love!' said Leo giving another laugh. 'If anyone had told me back then that the four of us would have been prepared to saw up, mince up and slice up – and did! – a nasty little teenage slut before putting him in a series of bags and then spending the next week or so depositing these in waste tips around this green and pleasant land, I would have sent for the men in white jackets!'

'IT'S ALL WORK RELATED'

Vincent stood eyeing his latest charcoal sketch, a smug, self-satisfied smile on his handsome, aquiline face. '*Perfetto,*' he murmured, 'absolutely fucking, wonderfully bloody perfect.' Placing the stick on charcoal onto the shelf of the easel he let out another satisfied sigh as, with eyes narrowing, he again surveyed the portrait of a fey young man, a local hairdresser and the darling of the moneyed matrons who lived in the well-heeled southern suburb of Richmond close to London. Derek Davis, for the moment a solitary figure on the large white paper block stood poised, smiling brightly, a hairbrush in one hand, a hairdryer in the other, as if about to weave the 'Lady D' (as he called himself) magic upon the head of yet another beaming customer.

'Now for your assassin, *queenie!*' announced Vincent with a smirk picking up the piece of charcoal again.

Vincent Carter (his mother having named him after the actor Vincent Price) described himself as an artist 'of the bizarre' but an artist still waiting to be recognized and now, with his latest planned series of portraits, about to become – in his mind's eye – more than simply recognized, but a twenty first century phenomenon. While waiting for the miracle to happen, Vincent – thanks to the aforesaid parent – was neither struggling or living in a garret, his version of a garret being a sumptuous studio flat in Glebe Place, Chelsea, just off the celebrated King's Road.

Vincent glanced back from the sketch to a news cutting carefully saved within a clear plastic folder and lying on a small table next to him. With his small, petulant mouth breaking into a self-satisfied smile a triumphant Vincent couldn't resist whispering, 'Like you, Gil Vincente, I now have *my* queen, the so-called Lady D, or more accurately, that piss drizzle Mistress Derek Davis, *the* most repellent little queen of them all! So, Gil Vincente, with one done and six to go this *other* Vincent, Vincent Carter, is about to stun London's glitterati gay world as it's never been stunned before!'

The news cutting in question referred to one Gil Vicente, a Brazilian artist whose self-portraits of him murdering a series of world leaders including, among others, the British monarch, President Bush and the Pope, had caused a storm at the Sao Paulo Biennial in September 2010. References to the outrage along with a photograph of the artist standing alongside several of his portraits had appeared in several of the major British papers, this particular article appearing in The Times.

Vincent, aged thirty two had – at long last – through the outrageous Gil Vincente, found his inspiration.

Charcoal at the ready he peered back at the news article. Yes Gil Vincente, he mused, The Queen was easy but where of where do I find my other six? Substitutes for a president, a pope, prime minister, arms dealer, a member of the military plus a celebrity for a laugh may prove a bit of a problem but one will and must prevail. Of course, with piss drizzle representing the queen and the others being made up of *queens I dislike,* it can only be the greatest gay art event London will have ever seen. Mark my words or – to be more precise – my portraits! Forget the money, honey! Those envious glances and bitchy comments will be even better than winning the fucking lottery!

Reaching for his morning vitamin shot – a tall glass of iced orange juice with a healthy dollop of Stolichnaya – Vincent stood in his usual balletic pose, his long feet encased in the de rigueur Gucci loafers, splayed out at the end of his long, thin legs, these being clad in a pair of tight black Dolce and Gabbana jeans. His skinny torso, shrouded in an extra-large white T-shirt, completed Vincent's perception of an artist at work.

'Yes, Derek drizzle Davis, you are a *perfect* substitute for the real one.' Vincent gave a snort. 'How is it you introduce yourself? Hairdresser to the stars? You fucking wish! Just because you once shampooed Helen

Mirren's hair when a junior at some celebrity salon in Mayfair back in the Middle Ages does not, my dear, make you a hairdresser to the stars!'

Taking a further sip of his drink he moved over to a high stool where he sat studying the solitary figure on the white sheet of paper. 'So, who else Derek dear?' he said aloud. 'Who else do I loathe enough to have them join you in my blood as well as charcoal bath?' Vincent, draining his glass, picked himself up off the stool and made his way over to the galley kitchen where a jug of vodka and orange juice, as opposed to a mere glass, was quickly prepared. Returning to the stool he pulled himself up back onto it before studying the smiling hairdresser once more.

'Oh but I'm really going to *enjoy* hurting you Derek Davis.' Vincent gave out a malicious snigger. 'Teach you to go around saying I only enjoy being fucked by someone sticking their *foot* up my arse! And on this occasion you weren't referring to a twelve inch dick!'

He looked down at the Gil Vincente article, now on his lap. 'Gill the Kill basically shows himself using a gun. Well, mega change number one, I don't possess a gun and two, I'm definitely going to be much, much more imaginative with my choice of weaponry. But whatever I use must be both artistic and symbolic; something also highly dramatic!' Vincent took a large final swig before replenishing his glass. 'But of course! Silly *moi*! Derek fucking Davis's demise can only be justified by a pair of scissors!'

Setting down his drink he moved back to his position in front of the easel. Three hours later a second figure, that of Vincent himself, stood behind the smugly smiling hairdresser, the same stance taken by Gil Vicente in his portrait with Elizabeth the Second. Unlike the Brazilian artist who held a gun, Vincent – arm raised – held a pair of scissors as if about to stab the unaware hairdresser in the back.

'Ouch! Fucking fab!' announced Vincent to the couple in the sketch, adding with a camp giggle, 'And what more appropriate way to celebrate such a satisfactory demise of queeny Derek, Lady D drizzle Davis, than a Kir Royale? So, Mr. VC and Senor GV, several Kir Royales coming up!'

That evening Vincent called Denny, a sporadic sexual partner who tolerated Vincent and his peculiarities simply for the lucrative benefits. Denny, a strapping, shaven-headed young man in his mid-twenties worked as a driver for a local haulage company. Much to Denny's amusement Vincent considered the rough and ready Denny more of a friend than a paid stud.

'Easy to be his best mate,' Denny would scathingly remark, 'especially when being his mate, or friend, means expensive gifts and liberal handfuls of cash!' The laughing young man had even confided to his regular group of trucker friends – the confession being received amidst disbelieving roars of laughter – 'Stupid cunt prefers sitting on my fucking foot instead of my cock and bouncing up and down while he wanks himself off!' More disbelieving laughter followed Denny's disclosure that he wore a size eleven boot.

'Denny, *c èst moi*! Are you free for a bite this evening? Cut the crap? Oh, you mean cut out my *Francais*! Oh Denny,' Vincent simpered coquettishly, 'I love it when you're so coarse, brutal and basic!'

'So you love it when I'm coarse, brutal and basic, do you?' came Denny's coarse, brutal and basic voice, 'Tell me something new!' Giving a harsh laugh he added, 'But why this evening, Vin? I'm already seeing you on Saturday.'

'I've decided to have an exhibition, an exhibition to be called' – here Vincent took a deep breath before announcing dramatically – '*It's All Work Related.*'

'It's all fucking work related?' came the sarcastic reply. 'Let's face it Vin the only work you're related to is either mincing off to a fucking cash point or writing the occasional cheque *or…*' here Denny gave out a lewd laugh, 'jumping up and down on my fucking foot!'

'Well that's all changed,' said Vincent primly. 'Today I finished – no, I *created* my first masterpiece and tomorrow I'm hoping to start the second.'

'Oh, and what's today's little err… *creation,* then?'

'It's a portrait of me and the Queen.'

'Pull the other one!' laughed Denny, 'or, in your case, *sit* on the other one!'

'I would like you to see it, Den,' cooed Vincent, 'I value your opinion!'

'*My* fucking opinion?' said the trucker, genuinely taken aback, his only idea of art being able to acknowledge the Tate Gallery when driving past. 'Tonight could be difficult,' he continued giving his co-driver Mike a mischievous wink, the two of them sitting in their local pub, a pint of lager each in front of them. 'Mike and me may have an unscheduled delivery to make and though *you* may not realize it Vin, no extra work means no extra treats, if you catch my drift.' Here Denny gave Mike another meaningful wink as he waggled the gleaming Rolex on his beefy wrist.

'When you say unscheduled I take it you mean it's not a regular company job?' came the terse voice over the static of Denny's mobile held out so both young men could listen to the selfish tone of the put out man. 'A bit of cash on the side I suppose?' Vincent added cuttingly.

'Err… yes, err… Vin. Times are tough at the moment,' mumbled Denny sounding suitably embarrassed while gesturing to a laughing Mike to quiet down.

'How much?' snapped Vincent.

Denny, after a moment or two's silence (apart from Mike's muffled laugher) named a figure causing even the laughing Mike to raise his eyebrows in astonishment.

'You're on,' said Vincent in an excited voice. 'Shall we say in an hour?'

'Eight hundred quid? Is the guy fucking mad?' questioned Mike as Denny handed him another pint.

'Fucking barking!' laughed Denny as he sat his large frame down alongside his friend. 'I'm supposed to give my fucking opinion on some fucking piece of shit he's *created*! *Created* for Christ's sake!' The big man took another healthy swallow. 'Stupid arsehole's now talking about a fucking exhibition! In all the months I've been visiting him I've never seen the poxy cunt working on a single painting!' Denny gave a grin. 'I don't think I've even *seen* a fucking painting!' Giving out a snort he couldn't resist adding, 'needn't have bothered to put on clean socks this morning, did I?'

'Filthy bugger!' guffawed Mike good naturedly.

'Oi! Watch it Mike! That's my foot you're talking about!'

'What do you think?'

'What do I think?' said Denny, a bemused expression on his weather-beaten face 'If you must know Vin, I think it's fucking marvelous!' which, to his surprise, the rough and ready man really did.

'I tell you Mike,' he said to his partner the next day as the two them travelled along the busy motorway en route to Manchester, 'the drawing was fucking good! It really was! I was really fucking amazed!'

'You say it's a sketch of him stabbing that hairdresser ponce with a pair of *scissors*?'

'Yes. Vin tells me he's been *inspired* or so he tells me – in fact he showed me – by this *other* Vincent's drawings, the other Vincent being a guy in South America who has just had an exhibition showing the artist himself killing a lot of world leaders and all that sort of shit. Our vindictive Vin is planning a similar exhibition here but using local gays as substitutes, local gays who've upset him in the past.'

'Where's he going to hold it then, Wembley fucking Stadium?'

'Not quite,' laughed Denny, 'so far he's only got seven in mind.'

'With Derek Davis standing in for the Queen?'

'Spot on!'

'Fuck me!'

'Later, if you're a good lad!'

'That'll be a shock for your cock having been of no use at all last night!'

'Oh? I eventually got a blow job for being my foot-*balling* skills!'

'Good for you!' laughed Mike. 'No wonder I was left to my beauty sleep when you got home.' He lit a cigarette which he passed over to Denny before lighting another for himself. 'So, who's next on the list?'

'Well, as he can't get the Pope he's going for that poof priest, the one who sometimes sneaks into our local and seems to think nobody recognizes him.'

'Ah yes, the one who calls himself Patrick and claims he's a travelling salesman of sorts.'

'That's the one, selling pharmaceuticals as opposed to God!'

'And how does Vincent the Second plan to assassinate this would-be pill pushing Pope?'

'Crowns the bugger with a crucifix!'

SIX MONTHS LATER:

Denny, accompanied by Mike, joined a mixture of gays (acquaintances as opposed to friends of Vincent's) along with a number of straights for Vincent's first curiously titled exhibition. On being interviewed – at a price – by a gay paper, Vincent's reasoning for his choice of the name, '*It's All Work Related*,' had been delivered with panache and quoted with malicious glee.

'Anything activating the imagination to pursue an objective, albeit designing a room, designing a dress, painting or sketching a portrait or even *contemplating an assassination* I simply say to those fortunate to have been so blessed, "Don't get on you high horse! Don't get above yourself! At the end of the day *It's All Work Related*!'"

Bathsheba Carter, Vincent's gregarious mother known as Ba to her friends, had dutifully brought along a group of loud, well-heeled, intrigued and bemused friends to the exhibition opening.

'I'm so proud of you, Vincent darling!' she crooned embracing her beaming son in several giant swathes of patterned chiffon, courtesy of Charles Svignholm, London's most exclusive fashion designer. 'And you look too, too divine even though about to commit such wicked, wicked deeds!'

Eyeing the tall, strapping figures of Denny and Mike standing like the giant Pillars of Hercules on either side of her skeletal son – both having 'dressed up' for the evening – in their neatly pressed open neck shirts and freshly pressed jeans showing of Denny's substitute foot to perfection (Mike's salami-like outline a close second), Bathsheba couldn't resist another ecstatic proclamation. 'And who are these two *gorgeous* hunks of testosterone? They cannot be *any* less than Messrs Universe and Wonderful!'

'Oh Mummy!' chortled Vincent on the highest of highs and completely missing the young men's amused glances at the word 'Mummy!' Unfurling himself from Bathsheba's possessive arms he gestured proudly at the two. 'This is Denny and this is Mike, my closest friends!' He gave a high pitched, excited giggle. 'It was Denny of course who encouraged me, gave me the final *push* as if it were to get this whole glorious, magical evening together!'

'How lovely, how... how *vivid*!' cooed Bathsheba before wafting off to join one of her friends but not before giving the two laughing young men a long perceptive look.

'Goodness Ba, I was wondering where you'd got to,' said Janice Ryder, the friend she'd quickly joined. 'Have you seen this?' she added, turning again to peer at the card pasted beneath Derek Davis's portrait. 'Certainly a most unpleasant title and an even more unpleasant drawing!'

'Oh?' said Bathsheba giving Denny and Mike another glance. 'Oh, and why is that Janice, dear?'

'Firstly I do think naming something *Killing The Queen* is not very nice, not nice at all, and furthermore this Queen's a man and, if I'm not mistaken, the spitting image of Derek Davis our local hairdresser, tiara or not!'

'Well then Janice darling,' cooed Bathsheba giving her friend a predatory smile, 'I can see you're positively *drawn*' – here she couldn't resist a tinkling laugh at her pun – 'so you simply have to buy him or her. I mean The Queen!'

'I must?'

'An investment, dear.' Bathsheba gave her friend a conspiratorial wink. 'I hear Vincent's been asked to exhibit a-b-r-o-a-d next!' she whispered before repeating the magical words. 'See it as an *investment*, Janice dear!'

By the end of the evening a jubilant Vincent proudly announced to Denny and Mike that all the drawings had been sold. To the young men's amusement Vincent seemed unaware the success of the sales had been totally due to the relentless actions of the tenacious Bathsheba. One such reluctant purchaser had been her 'man of the moment,' a scowling, very apparent homophobe, a ruthless City financier who was forced into buying a portrait titled *Killing Khashoggi,* Adnan Khashoggi being one of the most notorious arms dealers of the twentieth century. Here Vincent's substitute for the Turkish entrepreneur was the much disliked Anthony Grey, an antique dealer specializing in ancient weaponry. In the portrait the terrified dealer was shown on his knees, arms raised in surrender as a grim-faced Vincent faced him with a medieval crossbow.

Vincent, usually ignored by his fellow gays now found himself christened – as he later smilingly told Denny and Mike – with the exalted soubriquet, 'The Belle with the Balls!'

Shrieks of delight from certain of the more flamboyant guests greeted each drawing as the unpopular gay representative of the assassinator was recognized.

'Pity about the missing eighth!' came one high pitched shriek. 'But then these are strictly assassinations aren't they? Therefore not quite right to have had one of you-know-who committing suicide!'

Much later an exhausted Vincent lay between the still panting, sweat doused figures of Denny and Mike, each having satisfied Vincent with a vigorous foot fuck before jerking off over the whimpering, open-mouthed 'man of the moment', his head twisting violently as he gulped greedily in his efforts to catch their splattering cum.

Earlier Mike had watched in disbelief as the thin, thirty two year old, his eyes alight with an almost religious fervour, lowered himself slowly onto Denny's well-lubricated right foot until, along with the ankle and heel, it disappeared completely up Vincent's arse. Supporting himself with his own skinny arms placed firmly on the bed and with Denny gripping and lifting him by the shoulders, Vincent began to move up and down, bouncing rhythmically, his heaving movements gaining momentum.

'Jesus Den!' gasped Mike, his eyes wide.

'Yeah, I know what you're thinking, Mikey,' grinned Denny as he bounced the groaning Vincent with harder lifts and even harder downward pushes. 'Yeah, and you're bloody fucking well right! I *am* wriggling my fucking toes!'

'So Vince, what's next?' asked Denny as the three sat, drinks in hand, in the living area of the large studio, the two young men still naked while their host perched demurely in a brightly patterned Sulka dressing gown.

'I have no idea,' sighed Vincent moving his still tingling skinny shanks to make himself more comfortable on the large sofa. 'But no doubt inspiration will come.'

'Well, I certainly have,' sniggered Mike.

'And me,' laughed Denny.

'Touché!' giggled Vincent thinking of the endless slimy globules he had wiped from his chin and chest before voraciously licking his fingers clean.

There was a moment's contemplative silence before Denny asked quietly, 'Out of interest, how much did you make tonight, Vin?'

'Err... that's easy,' said Vincent giving the two young men a sheepish smile. 'Knowing West End prices, even though Fulham isn't the West End (the exhibition having taken place in a small gay gallery near upmarket Parson's Green) I put still put "silly bugger" prices on my drawings.' He gave another shy smile. 'I take it you didn't *look* at the prices?'

'No, we were too busy having a good time,' laughed Denny.

'Five,' murmured Vincent looking down at his bony bare feet.

'What, a lousy five fucking quid?' cried Denny, his eyes wide in disbelief.

'No, five *thousand* pounds,' giggled Vincent. 'Five thousand pounds per drawing.'

'Fucking hell!' whispered Mike.

'*Jesus* fucking hell!' gasped Denny.

Four days after the exhibition Denny called. 'Vin, it's Denny. Listen mate, Mike and I have an idea we'd like to put to you. You in later?'

Vincent, completely deflated, the euphoria following his brief taste of stardom well and truly forgotten immediately perked up, Denny having called *him* and not the other way round.

'You and Mike?'

'But of course! We're a threesome now, aren't we?' Denny gave a lewd chuckle. 'So, later OK for you?'

'Oh yes,' breathed Vincent. 'You'll stay for supper?'

'Supper *and* fucker!' laughed Denny crudely. 'But Vin, tonight it's business, proper business first before we get down to the other business!'

Two hours later a smiling Vincent greeted his two strapping guests.

'Another exhibition,' said Denny without further ado once the wine had been poured and the three were seated comfortably. 'But this time a series of high profile gays who have come out; politicians, pop stars, actors and all that sort of crap.'

'Another *assassination* exhibition?'

'A make believe one with the assassin this time being a cartoon figure. Like Mickey Mouse about to put George Michael's head in a giant mousetrap, the mousetrap on this occasion being an open toilet seat!'

'But that's pure *genius*!' breathed Vincent admiringly.

'Wait until you hear us out,' said Denny. 'This time you invite a mega crowd, straight, gay, blue or yellow, it doesn't matter and this time you hold the exhibition in a West End gallery.' The big man took another sip of his wine while a mesmerized Vincent looked on adoringly. 'You know that Ray Rogers?'

'The prehistoric PR queen?'

'That's the one, but prehistoric or not, a highly respected professional when it comes down to it.'

'So, what about this prehistoric professional?' asked Vincent cautiously.

'Well, Mikey and me, we've been fucking the arse off him over the past four months.'

'Oh,' said Vincent, his lips forming a tight line, a tinge of jealously running through his thin frame.

'C'mon Vin, you know us! Share and share alike! It's not as if we're a regular couple, or a threesome,' said Denny with a rough laugh. 'Whatever you may think, Ray Rogers is our man. He's the guy who can get the ball rolling as if it were. Hire you a prestigious West End gallery, get you all the publicity you need, the works. But Vin,' and here Denny leaning forward conspiratorially, Mike following suit, added in a theatrical whisper, 'there's more. Much more.' Having got Vincent's undivided attention he sat back. 'Oh, I know you can afford the basics Vin, the gallery, the *normal* PR Ray could get you, but as I've just said, there's more, much more that can be done.' Denny gave Vincent his most engaging smile. 'Believe me, with the money we could make with this exhibition, the all over costs – including Ray's fees – will be nothing more than mere fucking chicken feed!'

'What do I have to do?' asked Vincent tremulously but with a gleam in his eye.

'No no Vin, it's not what *you* have to do Vin, it's what we three are *going* to do.'

Three months later what should have remained another nondescript gallery opening regurgitated itself as front page news. The briefly reported murder of an insignificant gay hairdresser, a former employee of a prestigious Mayfair chain, having been plucked from obscurity thanks to the manifestations of one, Ray Rogers and given media prominence. 'Curiouser and Curiouser' ran the headline to the startling new piece written by a Rogers' associate, an article compelling enough to grab the public's ghoulish attention. *'Could Derek Davis,'* it began, *'a celebrity hairdresser found murdered in his Maidavale flat several days ago have been the result of an art exhibition staged at The Spaz Gallery in Fulham three months ago? Why? Because Derek Davis was one of the subjects of the exhibition and murdered in the same way as depicted in his portrait!'*

The article, vague in detail but heavy with innuendo soon caught the imagination of its readers. Was it simply a bizarre coincidence – as the Rogers' associate pointed out – Derek Davis had been stabbed to death by a pair of scissors? However, it was the final line which proved to be the pièce de résistance.

'Could this be the start to a series of copycat killings? Should the other subjects of the portraits be on the alert in case a similar fate befalls them?'

Two weeks later Father Edward Morrissey, aka Patrick the pharmaceutical salesman, was found lying dead behind the alter in his small suburban church, the murder weapon, a blood stained crucifix lying alongside him.

Ray Rogers went into overdrive. The priest's double life, the fact that he was a predatory gay and even more startling, the fact he had inadvertently appeared in Vincent Carter's recent sensational '*It's All Work Related*' exhibition, *the very same exhibition in which Derek Davis, the recently murdered gay hairdresser had also appeared, proved without doubt there was a connection. 'Will there be another?'* asked the wily PR man.

It was then that Ray gave out the even more riveting news; Vincent Carter was to hold a second exhibition, '*It's All Work Related Repeated.*'

'Could they stop the exhibition?' questioned Mike as the three sat discussing this latest gem of publicity.

'No,' answered Vincent loftily, 'See it as artistic freedom unlike the libelous, written word. I can assure you Mike, much more controversial displays have been seen in public art exhibitions here in London. Why, one artist even showed a faceless woman in a burka but with one tit exposed!'

'Need one say anymore?' laughed Mike.

'Whereas what we *do* need,' said Denny, 'is one more, preferably a few days just before the exhibition. That'll get them stampeding towards Cork Street!' (Cork Street being one of the most prestigious streets in Mayfair, famous for its exclusive art galleries).

'Anthony Grey,' said Vincent without hesitating.

'Fine, give us the details and we'll take care of it,' replied Denny, 'And tomorrow we're meeting your bank manager, right?'

'Absolutely,' said Vincent, 'and then we're lunching with my lawyer afterwards.'

The following evening Denny and Mike celebrated the day's events with supper at home in the bedroom of their untidy basement flat set in the salubrious downmarket area of Camberwell. Mike, having ordered in an Indian takeaway, saw the spicy meal along with several bottles of wine greedily demolished as the two lay side by side on the rumpled bed, their large frames propped up against the grubby headboard, a pornographic DVD flickering silently on the television while a local pop station played softly in the background.

'A good day if I may say so, Mikey,' said Denny giving the young man's heavy, flaccid uncut cock a squeeze. 'Imagine, a bank account which requires only two of three signatures to make any cheque or withdrawal valid?' He looked alongside at the lightly dozing Mike. 'Jesus Mikey, can you believe the dumb cunt? Furthermore, any future unsold works are the property of our new formed company and, if two of the three directors decide to sell any, they may do so at will! But what I find unbelievable is his agreement for the ownership of his studio being transferred to that of the company! That's you, me and Vin! However, I must admit I nearly shat myself when I thought that fucking lawyer was about to dissuade him!'

'Until he decided to take a piss at the same time as you!'

'Gobbled me down like a fucking turkey, he did! And in the Gentlemen's toilet of the fucking Ritz!' Vincent gave another disbelieving laugh and a tighter squeeze to Mike's slowly expanding cock.' Tell me Mikey, is our Vincent mad or is he merely bloody raving?'

'I've told you Den, it's simply our pedal power!' giggled Mike sleepily. 'He can't get enough of it whether he's sitting fucking side saddle; fucking riding it as if in the fucking Tour de France, or simply bobbing up and down like a some fucking demented cork on the bloody ocean wave!' He gave another soft giggle. 'No wonder I've got such a bloody sore ankle! That final little manoeuvre certainly required some persuading last night!'

'Your ankle and mine both!' laughed Denny. 'And what about this latest where he's asked us *not* to cut our fucking toenails for a week or two?'

'Well, for what we've achieved and about to receive I say we simply go on toeing the line!'

'Silly cunt!'

'Maybe, but the best substitute one you'll ever have!'

Anthony Grey's murder with a crossbow made the lead in most of the papers. *Vincent's Vendetta*? screamed one headline. *Vicious Vincent*! shouted another.

Vincent loved it!

Within the first hour of the private viewing all thirty drawings had been sold netting VDM, the new company's name, a staggering three hundred thousand pounds.

However, again the days slipped into weeks and the weeks into months and apart from a few interviews Vincent's name once again appeared to be sliding into obscurity. Several run-of-the-mill portraits had been taken on by the Cork Street gallery but remained unsold. The public had made it clear they wanted the assassination portraits and nothing else.

Four months later their patience was rewarded.

Billy Boy Bobski, a loud mouthed spotty teenager and pop idol, best known for his outrageous hit single *'I wanna walk your Tampax, I wanna be in you!'* – a rather incongruous choice for a self-professed extremely camp gay – was found dead in his luxurious Canary Wharf flat, choked by a mouth and throat stuffed full of Tampax. Needless to say this was the same method used for Billy Boy Bobski's demise in Vincent's portrait mischievously titled *'Eat Your Words.'*

Two more drawings already prepared in anticipation of the publics' reaction to this new piece of publicity were quickly placed in the gallery's window and sold within the hour.

'Another exhibition! We must have another exhibition,' cried an enthusiastic Vincent several days later having met up with Denny and Mike at the Glebe Place studio for another so-called business meeting. Had the 'artist of the moment' been less euphoric and not attending to replenishing their drinks he may or may not have caught the shifty glances passing between his two partners.

'You're absolutely right, Vin,' said Denny taking up the refilled champagne flute.

'Absolutely,' smiled Mike.

'Too dangerous,' said Mike, as he and Denny lay intertwined in bed later that night.

'We'll do one more, finishing up with five and then scarper,' said Denny giving his lover a firm kiss on the nose.

'Perfect,' said Mike before sliding his thick tongue into Denny's willing mouth.

Vincent's suicide was self-effacing to the last – he had swallowed a bottle of paint stripper – as was his suicide note left on the studio computer. *I murdered those men to promote myself as an artist supreme. I have no regrets and have enjoyed all the plaudits. How infuriating for all you collectors I never created the ultimate sketch! VC.*

After months of tense confrontation between Vincent's and Bathsheba's lawyers it was finally resolved that Denny and Mike were the legitimate owners of Vincent's multi- million pound spectacular studio. It took only a few weeks before the studio of the notorious portrait painter killer was purchased by a ghoulish multi-millionaire for – to quote a gleeful Ray Rogers – 'a substantial undisclosed sum.'

Denny and Mike eventually found themselves settling in Cape Town. After what they saw as a discreet period of 'allowing matters to cool down' they opened a gallery in the gay Waterkant district of the city, their speciality being landscapes by South African artists.

'Not much you can murder with a landscape,' Mike laughed as the two lay, lagers in hand, on adjacent sun loungers alongside the swimming pool set in the landscaped garden of their spectacular Constantia home.

'Don't knock it!' laughed Denny, 'You can always *bury* something in a landscape!'

A year later the local police were to be seen making a cursory enquiry into the disappearance of a local business man who, having set off on a business visit to Johannesburg had never arrived at his destination. No trace of the man meant to be flying from Cape Town International Airport – he had checked in but never boarded his flight – was ever found.

The man's business partner, Mr. Dennis (Denny) Halliday, had been quoted as 'devastated' by Mr. Michael (Mike) Powell's disappearance. The local press reported Mr. Powell as having intended to visit Johannesburg for the sole purpose of finding a suitable venue for a gallery to match their successful Cape Town operation. It had been planned to call the new Johannesburg gallery '*It's All Work Related Repeated*' after the Cape Town gallery '*It's All Work Related.*'

Future visitors to Denny and Koos's home (Koos Marais being a hefty blond, six foot four Afrikaner part-time rugby player and Denny's new business associate) were ritually shown a young Kaffir Boom or 'Lucky Bean' tree planted in memory of Denny's former partner, Mike. Several visitors were heard to comment admiringly on the vigorous growth of the colourful tribute.

CHOP PHOOEY

When asked the inevitable question by the cooing Miss Browning the twins' chirpy, chorused reply was simple and to the point, 'We're going to be celebrity TV chefs like that Jamie Oliver!'

'I'm going to be Jamie,' added nine year old James smugly.

'And I'm going to be his assistant and wear a big white hat!' chirruped his sibling, an equally smug Janet.

'How *original*!' said Miss Browning somewhat taken aback. In her day young boys dreamed of being policemen and little girls of being ballet dancers.

'And to show just how clever at cooking they are, today the twins made the sandwiches and baked a cake for our tea,' said their mother, blonde, vivacious, buxom Hattie Cooper as she stood smiling proudly at her offspring before adding, as a precautionary afterthought, 'It's cook' afternoon off.'

'How lovely,' murmured Miss Browning eyeing the two paragons gazing up at her, both blonde, both with big blue eyes and dressed identically in blue T-shirts and orange shorts. A second softer 'How delicious,' followed when viewing the plate of irregular size sandwiches, their sides oozing jam or relish plus a forlorn-looking cake (it had sagged hollowly in the centre) covered in a lurid, bright pink icing.

'So,' said Miss Browning before valiantly biting into a slice of the soggy cake, 'Mummy Hattie tells me it's your birthdays on Saturday and, as a special birthday treat you're being taken to *Mr. Wong*, your favourite Chinese restaurant in Chinatown! How *exciting*!'

'Yes, we like *Mr. Wong's*,' chirruped Janet, 'and so do Hattie and Jack.'

'Hattie and Jack?' questioned Miss Browning, not quite sure as to what she was hearing.

'Yes, or Mummy as you've just called her,' said James.

'Oh,' said Miss Browning.

'And David Mander our best friend is also coming,' added the beaming young boy.

'And I suppose he calls your parents Hattie and Jack as well?' said Miss Browning weakly.

'Oh no,' squeaked Janet reaching for another jam sandwich, 'David calls them Hats and Jacko!'

'How lovely,' murmured Miss Browning reverting to her reliable standby when at a loss for words.

'Yes, we like *Mr. Wong*,' said James, 'I like using the chop sticks.'

'I like using them for eating my spring rolls,' said Janet, determined not to be outdone by her twenty seven minute older brother.

'I like the seaweed,' said James as an afterthought.

'Me too,' cut in Janet, '*with* my spring rolls.'

'I must say it all sounds too, too heavenly!' said Miss Browning with an over bright smile. 'In my day we never had such exciting things to look forward to; a nice piece of ham and salad followed by bread and butter pudding was considered a very special treat.'

'That's because you're so old,' said Janet innocently while pinching her brother's leg under the table.

'Yes, ancient,' agreed James.

'Well *really*!' said Miss Browning.

'Yes, really,' said James.

Miss Browning lapsed into a tight-lipped silence while Hattie, giving her two smiling angels a beseeching look, carried on prattling inanely about the terrible weather and her observations on a recent film seen by her and Jack. To Miss Browning's increasing chagrin, Hattie appeared oblivious to the twins giggling and making faces at each other, blissfully content in their own private world.

'I nearly collapsed with laughter myself,' Hattie confided to Jack Thornhill, her burly stockbroker husband on his return from the office. 'Honestly Jack, if you could have *seen* Muriel Browning's face. Talk about not being amused! She's no doubt on the phone at this very minute to old Molly Wier about the terrible Thornhill twins!'

'Serve the old bat right,' laughed Jack, 'and she *is* old! Methuselah old! I won't actually say it to their faces but our twins aren't terrible at all, simply a pair of geniuses in the making. Him and her Einsteins! All thanks to clever Daddy Jack and yummy Mummy Hattie! Talking of which, where are the gruesome twosome?'

'Upstairs in the playroom.'

'Hmmm,' said Jack giving his wife a mischievous wink. 'What time's their supper?'

'The usual time so the answer is no, Casanova dearest, you'll simply have to wait!'

'Pity, I wouldn't have minded a quickie in an attempt to make another little Einstein!'

'Have a whisky instead,' laughed his wife, 'while thinking up delicious dirty thoughts for later!'

Had it been known Muriel Browning was on the phone and was talking to the aforesaid Molly Wier. 'Dreadful, dreadful little monsters!' she was saying before once again regaling her friend with the poor qualities of twenty first century parenting.

Meanwhile Miss Barling, an elderly spinster, had suddenly moved in next door having inherited the vast, sprawling Victorian neighbouring property from her reclusive bachelor brother. After a few days of her being in residence Hattie and Jack Thornhill were made to realize just how much the new inhabitant epitomized the phrase 'nosey neighbour.'

Jack, sunbathing alongside the pool with the twins, the three completely nude, had resulted in an immediate phone call from the affronted Miss Baring. Jack, having quite by chance picked up the portable phone lying next to his sun lounger had given the elderly woman short, sharp shrift.

'Tough shit, woman,' Jack had bellowed. 'If you don't like it, don't look! And mind your own fucking business! This is private property! Cunt,' he'd added before becoming aware of his children watching him with pure beatific delight!

'You *swore,* Jack!' giggled Janet.

'You said the S word, the F word *and* the C word,' whispered his young song in awe.

'I did, didn't I?' laughed Jack, 'but,' he added waggling a beefy finger at the grinning twins, 'that doesn't mean you can and don't you *dare* tell Hattie!'

A chastened Jack had confessed to an amused Hattie his outburst. 'Well worth it, though' he had added mischievously to his smiling wife, 'the twins loved it!'

'The twins heard you?'

'Of course! They lay there starkers alongside their well hung dad, egging me on!'

'Honestly Jack, at times…' giggled Hattie.

'Come to think of it Hats,' said Jack, a feigned look of puzzlement on his handsome face, 'maybe old Brownie has never *seen* a cock before and probably thought it was an invasion of the mighty anaconda!'

'Don't flatter yourself, husband dear! Python I'll accept but anaconda? In your dreams, lover boy, in your dreams.'

To validate her spinsterhood Miss Baring possessed the de rigueur cat, a mangy old tom called Mousey and an ancient Jack Russell terrier called Tigger. A source of great fun for the twins was to tease Tigger through a small, low level hole which had been mysteriously made in high wooden fence separating the two properties. James was convinced the hole had been made by a foreign spy whereas Janet firmly believed it had been made by a prisoner desperately trying to escape the vicious clutches of their former neighbour. The hole was, in fact, a former knot in one of the upright planks.

The twins had quickly learned how to tease the ancient dog, driving him to a yapping frenzy. This they did by taking it in turns to get down on their hands and knees so as to blow large farting noises through the aperture. James hated to admit it but Janet's wet farting sounds were far superior to his.

Teasing Mousey was even more fun. The ancient cat coveted a favourite sunbathing spot which again happened to be on a rockery adjacent to the dividing fence. It was here that Mousey could be found, weather permitting, lying supine like an old discarded grey woolen sock. It was at his twin's encouragement that James – the two having climbed up into an old Chestnut tree, part of which overhung the fence near to where Mousey was lying in a patch of dappled sunlight – pulled out his tiny penis (or pee pee pipe as his sister called it) and peed gustily over the sleeping beast.

A sopping, yowling Mousey had immediately fled back into the house via the open kitchen door where, seconds later (and to the twins' delight) a ready-to-do-battle Miss Browning had appeared, minus glasses, peering vaguely towards the clear blue sky. Changing direction she focused fuzzily on the distant fence, rockery and the overhanging tree where the two giggling children sat hidden amidst the thick foliage.

'I know you're there you horrid little beasts!' cried Miss Browning. 'If I ever catch you throwing water over my poor, defenseless Mousey again, I'll report you!'

Despite the threats Mousey remained the victim of endless golden showers with Miss Browning unable to prove the twins being responsible. When she did complain in person she was firmly told by Hattie that it couldn't possibly have been the twins. 'Janet and James simply *love* animals!' their doting mother had cried.

Needless to say a certain frisson remained between the neighbours until Hattie, always a generous soul and a firm believer in letting 'bygones be bygones,' had invited the dreaded Miss Browning to the special tea party where the twins would show what sweet and considerate little darlings they really were.

The birthday lunch was even more fun than anticipated, the fortune cookies at the end of the exotic meal – a formidable display of chopstick expertise by the twins and their friend – promising the three young guests 'good luck' and 'an unexpected surprise.'

A slow stroll through bustling Chinatown saw the potential chef and his assistants gazing spellbound in the windows of the colourful shops, eyes widening at the variety of hanging carcasses on display in the cluttered windows of the grocery stores.

Staring at the glazed poultry with their alarmingly orange-coloured feet plus the occasional piglet and rabbit, James, pointing to one nebulous hanging carcass asked curiously, 'Jack, is that one there a dog?'

'I think it's a cat,' ventured Janet.

'I think it's a baby,' sniggered David.

'All wrong,' laughed Jack, 'it's a goose, but minus its feet.'

'Very strange looking goose,' said James nodding his head affirmatively. 'I think David's right, it *is* a baby.' He gave his father a mischievous look. 'If *I* had a baby as ugly as that I'd definitely have sold it to the nearest Chinese grocery shop!'

'Don't be so wicked, Jamie!' laughed Hattie.

'But they *do* eat dogs and cats in China, don't they?' insisted Janet, more of a statement than a question.

'Maybe in China, Janet dear, but *not* in London,' said her mother firmly. 'Now, come along and look at those lovely cheongsams in that window over there.'

'I wonder what dog would taste like?' mused James.

'Well hopefully you'll never find out!' laughed his father. 'Now, come on you lot, Hattie wants us to look at pretty cheongsams as opposed to curious hanging bits of food!'

'I bet dog tastes awful,' said James giving the enticing window a final look.

In the car on the way home the young boy wouldn't let the subject drop. 'We eat chicken and meat,' he suddenly announced having sat silently while staring vacantly at the rows of terraced houses sailing past. 'So why not cats and dogs? They're also meat.'

'It's a nationality thing, Jamie,' said Jack looking at his son in the rear view mirror. 'For example people in South America eat guinea pig just as Eskimos eat raw fish.'

'Ugh!' exclaimed Janet, 'Mary Freeman has a guinea pig and I'd never eat that!'

'In China they also eat snakes,' commented Hattie enjoying the diversity of the conversation. 'While in South America they also eat alligator.'

'In Africa too,' said Jack caught up in the lively discussion, 'though of course they're called crocodiles there.'

'In France they eat frogs,' announced David determined to show he too knew something about the curious eating habits of the world. 'And snails!'

'Do they eat kangaroos in Australia?' asked Janet, her voice filled with indignation.

'It has been known,' laughed Jack. 'In fact there are several places in London where you can buy all these sort of strange food such kangaroo, crocodile and even caterpillars!'

'Caterpillars?' squeaked Janet. 'Ugh! Double ugh!'

'It's also known,' said Jack, giving his smiling wife a mischievous sidelong glance, 'that in certain parts of Indonesia and Africa too, I suspect, there still live those wicked cannibals!'

'Gosh!' exclaimed James with a broad grin, 'Real live cannibals?'

David, silent apart from his one earlier comment turned to Jack before clambering out of the car where Jack had stopped to drop him off. 'Do cannibals eat *everything,* Jacko?' he questioned, a frown on his young face.

'Everything,' said Jack with a grin.

'Unlike what's usually left on *your* plates!' chided Hattie with a laugh.

An excited James and Janet could hardly wait to get to James's computer. Several hours later Hattie knocked briskly on James's bedroom door. 'Supper in half an hour,' she called, 'and remember to wash your hands!'

Sitting round the large breakfast room table (meals on Saturdays and Sundays were always informal as opposed the more formal 'dinners' in the dining room during the week as served by Mrs. Horsfall, the cook) the twins happily relayed to their parents their discoveries on Google, the birthday apparently forgotten.

'They have recipes for kangaroo, crocodile, cats and dogs; all *sorts* of things,' said an excited James, adding, 'When I have my restaurant with Janet and David I'm going to serve up all sorts of animals and other things as well!'

'All sorts,' echoed his sister.

Three weeks later a distraught Miss Browning announced the sudden disappearance of her precious Mousey. Four weeks later the even more distraught woman announced the equally mysterious disappearance of Tigger.

Hattie, in one of her less doting motherly moments had confided her worst fears to Jack. 'You don't think the twins have anything to do with those damn animals disappearing, do you?'

'That's absolute nonsense Hats, and you know it! Janet and Jamie *love* animals.'

THREE YEARS LATER:

Instead of James's interest in becoming a chef being on the wane it had become an obsession. With Janet and the ever affable David the three had – much to Hattie and Jack's amusement – turned one of the old garden sheds into *James's Place,* a 'pretend' restaurant boasting two rickety tables and eight mismatched wooden upright chairs. Spurred on by his children's enthusiasm Jack had gone so far as to install a mini kitchen unit for the wannabe chef. The unit, a neat set of low level cupboards, contained a sink, small fridge, an oven and two electric rings.

'Keeps them out of mischief,' he assured an anxious Hattie, 'And don't worry about them forgetting to turn the oven or the rings off, I got Bert, the electrician to install a time switch. If anything *is* left on it will automatically be turned off at nine in the evening.'

'But what about perishables in the fridge?' asked the ever practical Hattie.

'For Christ's sake Hattie, they're still kids and it's only a make believe restaurant! If they're that worried about their fucking perishables there's a whole sodding top-of-the-range kitchen here in the main house at the little dears' disposal!'

The first official dinner hosted by *Jamie's Place* saw a bemused Hattie and Jack, along with David's parents, Daphne and Andrew, invited to *Jamie's Place* at six o'clock prompt to enjoy – according to a very self-important Janet – 'a gormit experience.'

To the surprise – and delight – of the four adults they were served a delicious 'Janet's soup,' followed by James's 'Day's Special,' a mouthwatering chicken and red pepper stew (the chicken breasts, at James's request, having been purchased by an amused Mrs. Horsfall a few days before).

The pudding course consisting of sliced pears in a sickly sugary sauce had been presented as 'David's Delight.'

Andrew Mander, David's father, having arrived carrying several bottles of wine for the grand occasion had said jokingly to his solemn-faced son, 'I take it there is a charge for corkage?' to which David, without blinking an eye answered, 'But of course Dad. That'll be one pound!'

Daphne Mander, not to be outdone but waiting until after dinner for her surprise gift presented the chef and his two assistants with an electric carving knife and a blender (the gifts having remained hidden in the kitchen of the main house until required).

'Oh, that's too, too extravagant, Daphne!' Hattie cried.

'Not at all, Hattie. They've sat in one of the kitchen cupboards for ages doing nothing else but growing whiskers! I must say I'm amazed, that dinner was really quite delicious! Chicken and peppers inspired by South America – or so David tells me! – I can hardly wait to see what *James's Place* offers up next!'

'Maybe a Kiwi roast of sorts, a leg of lamb which will be proudly carved by mine host using his new carving knife?' suggested Andrew.

'Don't be so ridiculous Andrew!' laughed Hattie, 'Leg of lamb is much too simple for James and his assistants, though by kiwi I take it you mean Jamie doing something clever with kiwi fruit?'

'Well, whatever,' muttered a suitably chastened Andrew.

THREE WEEKS LATER:

'What's the chef's special tonight, Jamie?' chucked Andrew Mander rubbing his hands in gleeful anticipation.

'Chop Suey,' announced the proud chef.

'That's Chinese, isn't it?' said Daphne Mander giving the twelve year old an indulgent smile.

'Yes,' said James solemnly standing alongside an equally solemn Janet and David. 'But like Jamie Oliver, everything we cook at *James's Place* is different. My Chop Suey is very special.'

'Well whatever, I'm sure it'll be delicious,' said Hattie firmly.

'I didn't want to say anything,' said Jack as the four adults made themselves comfortable in the study, after dinner drinks in their hands, 'But compared to their first attempt – that delicious chicken and pepper stew – I found tonight's offering more Chop *Chewy* than Suey!'

'Poor dears,' said Hattie, 'and they did try so hard, I mean imagine cutting all that pork into those delicate strips! Very time consuming! And not only that, 'she added, 'they refused to let Mrs. Horsfall do any shopping. The three insisted on doing this themselves *and* paying for everything out of their pocket money!'

'Whatever we may think,' said Daphne giving a placating smile, 'Like Hattie, I firmly believe David, like James and Janet, can do no wrong so, as far as they're concerned it's been another triumph.'

'Quite right, Daphne,' laughed Andrew, 'but I'll go one stage further than Jack and call it Chop *Phooey* as opposed to Chewy!'

'You *dare*!' shrieked Hattie as the others joined in laughing loudly.

Back in *James's Place* the three children sat at one of the tables – the washing and tidying up already taken care of – a Coca Cola each in front of them.

'We have to think up something less difficult next time,' announced James.

'I agree,' said Janet, a small frown crossing her forehead.

'Me too,' said David.

'Those hamburgers we made at your house and served to that stupid Richard and his friend were good and easy to make,' reminisced James.

'Even though that stupid dog was a bit difficult to mince so as to be mixed up in the proper mincemeat,' said David.

'Remember Richard's face when we told he's just eaten Tigger's minced pee pee pipe,' giggled Janet.

'Only he didn't believe us,' laughed James.

'And what about those pears we served last time to our parents?' snorted David. 'Me and Jamie peeing into the brown sugar to make the sauce!'

'What did you call them again?' sniggered Janet.

'*I* called them Piddling Pears but we told the grownups they were "David's Delight,"' snorted James.

'Pity the cat went bad,' sighed Janet.

'Yes, I liked the recipe on the website for roasted cat but then we forgot the fridge had been turned off and we didn't go near it for at least two weeks.'

'And pooh, the stink!' squeaked Janet. 'It was *awful* and the cat nothing else but slime!'

'And not possible to roast!' laughed her twin.

'We should have cooked those strips of meat much, much longer,' said James. Taking a thoughtful sip of his Coca Cola (as with the others, poured into a wine glass) James stared solemnly at his twin and his best friend. 'Yes, much, much longer. Jamie Oliver's word is simmer. We should have *simmered* more.'

'I wonder how long it'll be before someone notices old Miss Barling hasn't been seen around?' pondered David. He gave a sudden giggle. 'Didn't carving and chopping her up take ages?'

'And the mess!' exclaimed Janet, proof of her having inherited her mother's practical trait.

'Well, what we didn't use will never be found,' said David, his clear high voice full of confidence. 'The incinerator at school soon took care of that.'

'You looked so funny pushing that wheelbarrow full of black bags,' giggled Janet, 'and remember when Billings the caretaker asked what it was you wanted to burn and you told him Andrew had been clearing out the basement? Well, I nearly peed myself!'

'You didn't!'

'I did! In fact my knickers were quite wet!'

'Girls' pee? Ugh!' said David with an exaggerated grimace. 'How nasty!'

'Isn't it sad,' said James quietly showing little or no interest in sister's and David's banter, 'Isn't it sad,' he said again more loudly in order to gain their attention.

'What's sad?' asked Janet eyeing her brother curiously.

'Sad our parents – Jack especially – will never know they're now cannibals,' said James in a disappointed voice before letting out an equally disappointed sigh.

'I COULDN'T POSSIBLY RUN ON COBBLES!'

Tamara Tagata (pronounced Ta-*garter*) stood fuming by the bus stop, her faux leopard skin coat drawn tightly around her thin shoulders, her high-heeled red suede pixie boots viciously pinching her large feet.

'So much for fucking Cinderella,' she griped, giving her friend Bella Donna – as wide as Tamara was narrow and short as Tamara was tall – the filthiest look she could muster before turning away and glaring at the torrential rain.

Tamara (real name George Talbot) and Bella (real name Donald Biggles) had met an hour earlier at their usual Friday evening rendezvous, Kip's Place, a private transvestite club in London's supposedly notorious Soho. George, a senior accountant by day with the prestigious firm of *Sharp, Sharp and Collick,* would rush home each Friday, shower and within a self-pampering hour transform himself (so he believed) into the alluring, tantalizing and irresistible blonde siren Tamara Tagata.

Likewise Donald, a partner in a chain of successful florists, *Flori-Abundance of Mayfair,* would religiously follow a similar performance transforming himself into the delicious and desirable (as he too believed) Bella Donna.

'Feet hurting, dear?' simpered Bella, a mischievous smile on her cerise-coloured lips as she looked up at her grim-faced friend. 'I *told* you to order two sizes larger but no, as per usual, Miss Tamara Tagata always knows best.'

'Two hundred quid literally going down the fucking drain,' scowled Tamara. She glared out at the rain sheeting down outside the non-effective bus shelter. 'Next time Miss Donna we take a fucking taxi,' the furious lady snarled.

'*Excuse me*!' said Bella, her voice ringing with indignation. 'Who, may I ask suggested we grab that taxi we saw when we came out of Kips's? And who said it a waste of money? I quote "the bus stop is just across the street?" Just across the street? (Bella's voice had now risen to a screech) Bloody fifty yards *down* the street!'

'Speak of the devil,' said Tamara smugly as a large red double-decker appeared around the street corner. 'See, there *is* another god as opposed to this fucking rain one!'

Sitting themselves firmly in the only two seats available – the sign 'Priority Seats – Please give up these seats for a Disabled Person,' prominently displayed alongside – the two sat staring stonily ahead. It took only a moment before Tamara became aware of several loud sniggers coming from behind them. Turning her blonde head sharply (tonight adorned by an Ivana Trump-style beehive) Tamara looked straight into the mocking eyes of a handsome young man in his late teens sitting alongside his equally mocking companion, both still at college or at school but out for a night on the town.

Giving another snigger the youth turned to his smirking friend. 'I think it fancies me, Nige! Fancies me rotten!'

The spotty-faced Nige, or Nigel, emboldened by his friend's snide remark gave Tamara his idea of a lewd wink. 'Problem is my friend charges to fuck your sort!' he giggled.

Tamara's reaction was to give the two young men a look of pure venom resulting in the smirking Nige having to look away while clearing his throat nervously, his anonymous companion eventually being forced to do the same. To their increasing discomfort Tamara, instead of turning back and looking stonily ahead as before, continued staring at the two, eyes unblinking.

'Err... look, I'm sorry err... Miss,' stammered the one called Nige somewhat alarmed by the staring Medusa-like figure in front of him (Tamara's beehive having started to unravel serpent-like in the rain). 'And

I err… apologize for my friend. We were only having a bit of a laugh,' he added lamely, his voice trailing off into a mere whisper.

Tamara remained silent, her look of pure hatred unwavering.

'Oh shit!' muttered Nige. Turning to his equally uncomfortable friend he hissed, 'For Christsake Tim, apologize to her, it, whatever and let's get the hell out of here!'

'Sorry *sir*!' spat out Tim in a flash of bravado as he started to rise from his seat.

'Sorry *sir*?' purred Tamara, eyes still unblinking. 'Oh no, Tim Collick, you and your friend shivering next to you, that walking piece of acne Mr. *Nigel* Carpenter, haven't the remotest idea as to what *sorry* can really mean.'

'You know our names?' gasped the teenager identified as Tim.

'And your addresses!' said Tamara, the former purring now a snarl as the visibly shaken teenagers slowly drew themselves to their feet in anticipation of the next stop, their nervousness increasing as Tamara herself started to rise up from her own seat.

'What are you doing? It's not our stop?' said Bella.

Turning to look down at her seated friend Tamara said in her best baritone, 'Enough is enough! We've done it before and there's no reason why we shouldn't do it again. I plan to beat the shit out of these two pathetic cunts! Whether you join me or not it's entirely up to you!'

Without hesitating Bella stood up.

As soon as the bus drew to a halt the two teenagers made a dramatic dash for the door, pushing their way through the other passengers and disappearing into the rainy night.

'Aren't we going to follow them?' asked Bella as Tamara stood staring at the still open door.

'No, not this time,' said Tamara sitting down again. 'They've obviously run down that narrow alley behind the stop and besides, wearing stilettos I couldn't *possibly* run on cobbles!'

'Cobbles? What cobbles?'

'The alley way, Bella, it's all cobbled!'

'I can't see any sodding cobbles!' cried Bella attempting to peer out of the darkened window and seeing only her reflection.

'That's because we've now *left* the bloody bus stop,' hissed Tamara as if speaking to a halfwit. 'In case you've forgotten we're trundling through picturesque Marylebone and there are an awful lot of little cobbled nightmares leading off from this main thoroughfare so there's no point in trying to chase the little bastards!'

'Ooh, get her!' sniped Bella adjusting her spangled skirt above her plump knees. 'But tell me, she who doesn't run on cobbles, what did the kid actually *say* to get your knickers in such a twist? I haven't seen you quite so pissed off for a long time! But more importantly, how on earth did you know their names?'

'That Tim Collick, his father's chairman of the accountancy firm I work for. I've often seen the little twerp in the office along with little twerp number two, master acne advert. *His* name is Nigel Carpenter and his father's one of the company directors.

Bella couldn't resist a snigger. 'Just as well they didn't recognize the suave Mr. Talbot!' resulting in another of Tamara's venomous glares. 'Oops! Sorry dear,' said the solid, barrel-like little man with a laugh. 'I mean *nobody,* but nobody, could or would associate the glamorous Tamara Tagata with the nerdish George Talbot, account bore supreme!'

'Could I suppose somewhere deep, very deep within that shitty remark there may just lurk a very remote form of a compliment?'

'Yes, your talent for sleuthing never fails to astound me,' laughed Bella. 'But tell me, super sleuth, what did the little cunts say to spark you off like that?'

Tamara quietly repeated the vindictive comments made by the two boys.

'Little cunts!' muttered Bella (cunt being her favourite four letter word), adding, 'We're here. Come on, Miss T. I think we both could do with a very stiff drink to start with and hopefully, something even stiffer afterwards!'

The quiet, hardworking George Talbot was known in his office as a recluse, his only interest apart from his work being an inexplicable passion for karate.

'Talk about never judging a book by its cover!' Pam, his devoted secretary had been heard to say on numerous occasions. 'Why, he's even won several awards for martial arts!'

'Forget the bloody martial arts,' George would laughingly say to Donald when reporting the latest burst of accolades from Pam. 'Imagine Pam's face if I told her I'd won the title of *Miss Super Tranny, Birmingham,* twice?'

While George devoted himself to karate Donald's other passion was billiards and, like George, boasted several gleaming trophies to prove his expertise in the game. 'Touché,' had been Donald's quick riposte, 'and imagine the staff's reaction at *Flori-Abundance* should they ever find out the butch, tough Danny DeVito lookalike, their very own very precious, rarest of hot house plants, Mr. Don Biggles, likes wearing sequinned cocktail frocks and a Farah Fawcett wig along with the most outrageous "fuck me" pumps when painting the town pink every Friday night with her best girlfriend, Tamara Tagata!'

The two had met at the first *Miss Super Tranny* competition, Donald coming third to George's first. The two had become inseparable friends.

Soon after they had met Tamara and Bella had been subjected to a similar incident similar as the one experienced earlier in that evening. On this occasion the three youths subjecting the two friends to a barrage of jeers and insults had found themselves severely beaten up by the 'fucking tranny freaks,' resulting in the three being taken to the A & E of the local hospital, two with broken jaws and ribs and one with a broken nose and broken collar bone. Needless to say the three louts had been too embarrassed to put in an official complaint to the police.

'Those two *have* well and truly pissed you off this evening, haven't they?' stated Bella as they sat sipping their third large vodka and tonics while watching the colourful crown of trannys, dykes and gays chatting happily around them.

'Totally,' said Tamara. 'It's not often I get so niggled but those two should know better! Furthermore, half the bloody employees at Sharp, Sharp and Collick are fucking gay even though they're mostly closet cases!'

'You exaggerate?'

'Well, maybe a couple.' Tamara gave a hollow laugh. 'Take Miss Henderson for example, bloody Tim's father's secretary. Now there's a prime example of a thundering diesel dyke!'

'So, what are you going to do about it?'

'Do about it?'

'Yes dear, *do* about it! If I recall and despite all these vodkas I've been pouring down by greedy gullet in lieu of you-know-what, your very words to those two were they hadn't, and I quote – "the remotest idea as to what sorry can mean," – unquote.'

'I did?'

'You most certainly did.'

Tamara gave a mischievous smile. 'Well then Miss Donna, may I suggest we somehow prove to them the person speaking in jest wasn't jesting?'

'Why not, Miss T? Another large v and t to seal the deal?'

'Why not, Miss B?' Tamara gave a mirthless laugh. 'Some fun fucking Friday this is turning out to be. Tell you what Bella dear, let's have one for the road and then make tracks. I'm not really in a cruising or bruising mood!'

'Nor I.'

'So let's go back to *Maison* Tagata – in a *taxi* this time – crack a bottle of wine or two, maybe even three. Who knows we may even get pissed enough to fuck *each other*!'

'You're on!'

'Thank Christ for that! And, as you may have guessed, I can't *wait* to get these fucking shoes off!'

THREE MONTHS LATER:

George, in between dictating a letter to the ever-attentive Pam, glanced up at the two figures walking past the glass partition separating his office from the main accountancy area.

'George?'

'Err... sorry Pam, lost the plot for a second! Where were we?'

Pam dutifully read back the last few words.

'Of course! So, let's continue...In return...' George began, taking up from where he had left off. Within a few seconds he'd forgotten the brief glimpsing of Tim and Nigel obviously on their way to Tim's father's office.   Minutes later, a second glimpse of the laughing two along with a beaming Mr. Collick on their way out to lunch or some other engagement, immediately brought back to George's mind his and Donald's conversation several months before.

The sight of the two arrogant teenagers and their patronizing grins at the junior employees huddled over their desks caused George to take a deep, calming breath before picking up his mobile and quickly punching in a number.

'Good morning, is Donald Biggles about? It's George Talbot. Ah, Janet, I thought it might be you! Now tell me, how *is* the prettiest blossom in the shop this morning?' Peals of delighted laughter followed George's regular greeting before Janet, a large, jolly Jamaican woman and longstanding receptionist at *Flori-Abundance,* went to find Donald.

'Don, me. Remember those two little shits on the bus several months ago, smug arse one and smug arse two? Well, I've just seen them leaving the office with daddy, or smug arse senior, obviously on their way out to lunch or something. Remember our oath sealed by that final vodka and t? Good. So instead of a jest let's make it a quest!'

'Pam, those two young men in here earlier – the two who went out with Mr. Collick – was that young Tim? If it was, God how he's grown!'

'And ever so handsome and so, so charming!' gushed Pam, a matronly forty year old. 'Honestly George, if I was a young girl again I certainly would have cast my eye his way!'

'Only your eye? Oh, come off it, Pam! From what I've heard about your racy past it would more than likely have been your knickers!'

'Oh George! You are so *wicked*!' giggled a delighted Pam, turning bright pink at George's mischievous quip. 'What would my Andrew say if he ever heard you suggesting my past was nothing less than perfect?'

'Andrew would more than likely say, "You're right George, that's why I married her! *Because* she wasn't perfect!"'

More giggles and delighted wriggles greeted this latest bon mot.

'Seriously Pam, where *do* all the youngsters like Tim and his friends go these days, especially on a weekend? *I* mean I like to go out on a Friday for an occasional drink, maybe the Ritz or Claridges if I'm really splashing out, but where do all the kids go?'

'Oh, I know Tim and his equally charming friend Nigel – that's Nigel Carpenter, Mr. Carpenter, one of the senior partners' son – are great habitués of that popular club in Earls Court, The Troubadour. Apparently it's a favourite of Prince Harry. Tim and Nigel are always there. In fact young Tim was raving to Rose, Rose Henderson, his father's secretary, about a recent event held there, a tribute to Jimmy Hendrix. According to young Tim it was quite something.'

Since when would an old dyke like rugged Rose be interested in the music of Jimmy Hendrix thought George but said instead, 'Ah yes, I know The Troubadour. Many a great has played there, among these Eric Clapton, Bob Dylan and Paul Simon to name but a few.'

'That's the place,' smiled Pam. 'Quite a little raver on the quiet, aren't you George,' she added with another giggle.

A few minutes George was on the mobile to Donald. 'You ever heard of The Troubadour, Don?'

'But of course. Wild and very popular spot. Good music, great food and a fabulous ambience both upstairs and downstairs, the downstairs being where they have this great club.'

'You've *been* there?'

'Yes dear, several times and – are you sitting down on that little abused arse of yours? – always as the always lovely and breathtaking Bella Donna!'

'You went in *drag*? George's voice was incredulous.

'Darling, put it this way, I wasn't the only tranny on the town those nights!'

'Can we go there this Friday?'

'What, as George and Donald or as T and B?'

'How is it, Donald dear, that only *you* can make us – when all gussied up – sound like a disease?' laughed George, 'Yes, as T and B.'

'I don't see why not. Tell you what, I'll give them a call and see what's happening in the club on Friday.'

'Irrespective of what's going on, were going to be there this Friday and every consecutive Friday until we've completed our quest.'

Three Fridays later Tamara and Bella found themselves seated at a small table in the noisy basement club, their own table placed a few tables away from where Tim and Nigel were sitting accompanied by a mixed group of loudly laughing and shrieking friends.

'Watch this,' whispered Tamara slowly putting down her drink and fixing a laser-like glaze on the laughing Tim. It only took a few minutes before the young man, a puzzled expression on his handsome face, gave a flickering glance around the crowded club, his face freezing as he was caught up in Tamara's stony gaze. Giving a visible gulp Tim turned his head sharply towards a guffawing Nigel. Unable to catch his friend's attention he lent across the low table and grabbed Nigel roughly by the arm.

'What?' mouthed Nigel.

'They're here!' shouted Tim, his words lost against the amplified music.

'What?' mouthed Nigel again, a bemused look on his face.

'They're here!' screamed Tim gesturing wildly at Tamara and Bella's table.

'Who are here?' shouted Nigel, his voice loud and clear as the curious group, now silent, sat staring at a wild-eyed Tim.

'Those fucking trannys,' hissed Tim, his voice level almost back to normal. 'Over there at the small table alongside the column.'

'What are you on, Timmy?' giggled one of the girls in the group. 'The table next to the column is empty!'

Tim, after a second sighting of Tamara and Bella at The Troubadour followed again by their sudden disappearance, found himself surreptitiously looking around for the two trannys irrespective of where he might be.

'Jesus, Tim,' snapped Nigel one lunchtime on seeing Tim casting several nervous glances around the large room glamorous diners as the two sat in their favourite London West End eatery, The Wolseley. 'What the hell's the matter with you? OK, OK, so we just happened to see those two fucking trannys again at The Troubadour the other night.' He let out an exasperated sigh. 'Has it occurred to you they may even *like* the music there, may even like the club, the whole thing?'

'They're after us.'

'Bullshit! If I didn't know you were fucking Emily Cooper every fucking morning, noon and night I'd say it's *you* who's after *them*!'

'Who are you bringing to the Christmas party, George?' asked Pam. 'Some mystery blonde?'

'When I secretly lust after you and can't wait to get you under the mistletoe? Come off it Pam, why on earth would I need a substitute blonde?'

'You are so, so wicked!' squealed Pam going her regular pink. 'I keep telling you I'm a happily married woman!'

'Knickers to that!' laughed George, his comment being received with further delighted squeals.

'Actually I'm bringing another potential client. Mr. Collick, as you know, encourages us to invite any, quote – "person or persons who may be of benefit to the company's wellbeing" – unquote. The icing on the Christmas case as he also puts it.' George gave a self-effacing laugh. 'Ever since I inadvertently brought along Anthony Broadstairs that one Christmas and we got the Broadstairs account...'

'A *mega* account!' said Pam interrupting.

(Yes, thought George, and I wonder what you would say, Pam dear, if you knew the erudite Mr. Broadstairs spent most of his weekends queening it up around his country estate while in the guise of the aristocratic Antonia Amore!)

'OK, a mega account; ever since then Mr. Collick seems to think it's *my* Christmas treat for the company to deliver up another Anthony Broadstairs! Hopefully Donald Biggles will turn out to be this year's gift.'

'Donald Biggles?'

'*Flori-Abundance*. Ring a bell?'

'The chain of high class florists? But of course!'

'There you are then.' George gave the smiling woman a lascivious wink. 'Maybe or maybe not I could be getting a *mega* discount on all those dozens of red roses I could be sending a certain P-A-M next Valentine's Day!'

'Promises, promises,' giggled Pam.

'And the son will definitely be at the Christmas bash?'

'Has been for the past three years. As has his soulmate, the Carpenter boy.'

'So what do we do?' Donald gave snigger. 'Surely you're not planning to turn up at the Christmas do in drag, are you? Joke, Geo! Joke!'

'No, not there, later and *this* is what we're going to do.'

For the annual Christmas get together for both clients and staff, Sharp, Sharp and Collick religiously hired the ballroom of a five star West End hotel. The event, a 'no expenses spared' affair was seen as a 'thank you' to the hardworking members of the firm and a particular thank you to the wealthy and influential clientele making up the company's impressive portfolio. Mr. and Mrs. Collick, both sticklers for tradition, insisted on a dress code of dinner jackets and evening dress.

'Pity we *can't* go as our alter egos,' camped Donald. 'I've just bought *the* most divine cocktail number in mauve tulle and mauve sequins!'

'Just as well,' replied George drily.

'You're young Mr. Collick, aren't you? George, George Talbot, I'm one of the senior accountants.'

'Oh, Mr. Talbot! Yes, Dad has mentioned you.' Tim gave out a braying laugh. 'If I'm correct he refers to you as the man with the fishing line! You always manage to pull the big one in! Ha ha ha!'

'Your father said that?'

'He did indeed, Mr. Talbot.' Tim leant forward, whispering confidentially. 'It's not official as yet but obviously one day I'm going to be taking over the company from Dad and so he's err... grooming me as if it were. Soooo, yours truly here already knows a great deal – if you catch my drift – about some of the ins and outs of the firm and you're definitely one of the *ins*! Ha ha ha!'

'Good heavens,' said George looking at the smirking charmer. 'Good heavens,' he muttered again. 'Well, thank you for the *in*sight err... Mr. Collick.'

'Oh, Tim please, *George*. After all, I'm not your boss, *yet*! Ha ha ha!'

'I look forward to that err... Tim.' He nodded to where Donald was talking animatedly to Anthony Broadstairs. 'Somewhat of a coincidence you telling me what you dad calls me. See that gentleman talking to Anthony Broadstairs?'

'I do indeed,' said Tim. 'I mean, I see a midget sumo wrestler lookalike and Mr. Broadstairs! Ha ha ha!'

'Well, sumo or no sumo your probably looking at the next big company account.'

'Really? Dad will be pleased.'

Really? Thought George, Really? Oh, you obnoxious braying little prick, you're even worse that I remembered. And I very much doubt if your equally as obnoxious daddy will be *really* pleased at all!

Catching Donald's eye (Donald having kept glancing towards George while waiting for his signal) the short, thickset man excused himself from Anthony and made his way over to join the two.

'Hello again, George,' said a beaming Donald. 'And this gentleman is...?'

'Tim Collick, our chairman' son.'

Introductions made and with a polite, stilted conversation ensuing it was Donald who suggested a break for a cigarette. 'Such a bore this ban on smoking in public places,' he griped.

'Hear! Hear!' brayed Tim.

'As it's not too cold out fancy a stroll?' asked George. 'There's a small mews which runs alongside the hotel where we can have a smoke plus' – here he gave his two companions a wink – 'a pub if a smoke *and* a drink appeals. And don't worry about the dinner jackets; they're quite used to us nicotine-addicted desperados sneaking in from various functions for a celebratory drink after those first few satisfying puffs!'

'Would you mind if I asked Nige to join us?'

'Nige?'

'My best friend. Nigel Carpenter. His dad's another of your bosses. The guy standing over there.'

'Why not,' said George avoiding Donald's glance following the 'another of your bosses' remark, 'the more the merrier.'

TWO DAYS LATER:

'Let us out! Let us out!' screamed Tim hoarsely, banging his bleeding fists against the locked door. Turning he glanced at the huddled heap of his sniveling friend. 'For fuck's sake Nige! Quit with the histrionics! We've got to get ourselves out of here!'

'What happened?' gasped Nigel, choking on more tears and wiping his eyes, 'what's happening to us?'

'Jesus, Nige! I've already *told* you I don't fucking well know! I don't even fucking well *remember*!' yelled Tim. 'All I *do* remember is having a drink outside a pub with a couple of guys from the party and then they left us, saying they had to get back.' He looked curiously at Nigel who was looking up at him with a look of growing disgust on his tear streaked face. 'Now what?'

Nigel left out a small groan, 'I think I've just shat myself!'

'What else, Nige, what else?' said Tim in a frightened whisper.

'It hurts… I'm sore… '

'Jesus!' Tim, his face as pale as his friend's muttered, 'Your belt, Nige. Have you got your belt?'

'I think so, I don't know… why?' asked Nigel in a shaky voice, fumbling for the top of his trousers.

'Nige, I'm missing mine and I think you'll find yours is missing too.'

'No, it's not here,' whimpered Nigel.

'Nige,' whispered Tim, his voice trembling, 'I think we were both drugged and err… oh shit, Nige, I think we've both been drugged and *fucked*!'

Nigel's only reaction was a low moan accompanied by a very wet, dribbling fart.

'Nige, take of your trousers and check your underpants. No, no, now's not the time to be embarrassed. I did the same as you earlier, shat myself. I took off my underpants but couldn't help noticing there was more blood and err…what I think was cum as well as shit.' Tim gave a gulp. 'I wasn't going to say anything thinking maybe it was only me but now it's the two of us…' he whispered, his voice faltering.

'But how? When? Where?' croaked Nigel moving his body uncomfortably as another dribble of blood, cum and shit made its presence known.

'As I've already said Nige, I don't know, I really don't know,' whispered Tim, 'but I think this is only the beginning.'

Nigel, now standing holding onto Tim, looked at his friend's equally horror-stricken face as they suddenly became aware of a key turning in lock to the door.

'Good evening gentlemen,' said Tamara Tagata, resplendent in a gold sequinned cocktail dress and the original Ivana Trump blonde wig.

'Good evening gentlemen, 'echoed Bella Donna, equally as resplendent in a sequinned frock of mauve tulle and matching sequins.

'So, Tim Collick,' said Tamara with a lascivious scarlet grin. 'You said I fancied you, did you? Well, you got it wrong sweetheart, I didn't fancy you but that didn't stop me fucking you! Three times to be exact not counting the three times by my friend Bella here and the other countless times with a billiard cue.' A still smiling Tamara turned to Nigel making a pathetic attempt to hide behind Tim, a dribble of blood and shit having trickled down the inside of one trouser leg and now glistening on his bare foot. 'And as for you, *Nige,* sadly your friend's "sorry, *sir*" wasn't sorry enough so, on behalf of "sorry, *sir*" you too were fucked six times – three times by me and three by Bella – but *Nige,* oh Nige, how you screamed when we fucked you and Timmy boy simultaneously time and time again with *two* separate billiard cues! As Bella said, after two days of ramming those cues up your arses she's amazed there's anything *left* of the cues, never mind your arseholes!'

A heavy silence fell upon the basement room.

'Cat caught you tongue, Timmy dear?' Tamara finally hissed, giving the two terrified boys a syrupy smile as they stood clutching each other, staring wide-eyed at their two tormentors. 'Well, I'll tell you what Timmy, now we've finished fucking you – by the way, nasty flabby arse, kiddo, you should have exercised more! – we're about to beat the shit out of you! And this is how we're going to do it! Me? – I'm Miss Tamara Tagata by the way and little Miss Muscle over there is Miss Bella Donna – me? I'm going to hand chop and kick you about for starters then the other – again I quote "fucking tranny" unquote – is going to beat the shit out of you with one of the surviving billiard cues. And after all that' – here Tamara gave a queenly laugh- 'who *knows* what these fucking trannys will think up next!'

'Noooo!' screamed Tim as he made a desperate lunge for the open door, his beltless trousers meanwhile falling down, tripping him up and causing him to slam headfirst into the door jamb.

'No you don't' yelled George, his Tamara persona forgotten, as he grabbed Tim by a flailing arm. Spinning the young man round he gave him a resounding backhander across the face.

'My turn!' yelled Donald, his Bella persona also forgotten. Skillfully wielding his billiard cue like a fighting staff he gave the screeching Nigel a resounding thwack across the face causing his nose and left cheek to cave in with an audible crunch.

Three days later the bodies of two transvestites were found partially hidden in a deep thicket on the notorious Clapham Common, a well-known cruising area for gays. The general reaction was one of shock combined with a ghoulish fascination, the interest in the two deaths reaching to a frenzied state when the identities of the victims were made public. Not only were the two young men the sons of both the chairman and a managing director of the prestigious Sharp, Sharp and Collick accountancy firm, but given the additional facts both had been sexually abused and brutally beaten while dressed in a pair of garish cocktail dresses, their faces grotesquely made up and a pair of cheap wigs stuck on their battered heads, the press had a field day.

Among the mourners paying their respects at the two funerals was the quiet, self-effacing George Talbot.

'I'm so sorry about your tragic loss, Mr. and Mrs. Collick,' he had said in his most sympathetic tone at funeral number one.

'I'm so sorry about your tragic loss, Mr. and Mrs. Carpenter,' he had said in his most sympathetic tone at funeral number two.

'We're not the least bit sorry, are we Bella dear?' said Tamara Tagata George at Kips's the following evening.

'Not at all, Tamara dear,' said Bella Donna Donald, 'but as you say, we're never *ever* taking a bus again!'

The plan had proved to be perfect, Donald having borrowed one of the many *Flori-Abundance* delivery vans that afternoon and parking it discreetly on a delivery bay close to the pub in the mews adjacent to the hotel. They had left Tim and Nigel holding a large vodka and tonic each – George's round – liberally dosed with GHB. Waiting alongside the van now in deep shadow they quickly went to the assistance of the two young men stumbling about in a drugged daze. Having bundled the two into the back of the van (both had put on surgical gloves which would be constantly changed over the next few days) they drove silently back to Donald's small cottage in Wimbledon village. For two days and two nights the victims, constantly sedated, were brutally fucked, fisted and fucked again with a pair of billiard cues. It was only after the second sex session that Donald has pointed out neither had been wearing condoms.

'Bit late,' laughed George. 'However, I can't see any reason why we should ever have to give a DNA sample. I take it you never have, Bella dear?'

'Don't be so vile Tamara! Surely you must be aware our very personal DNA deposits are strictly family! One can forget the occasional strays.'

The final act of revenge had been allowing Tim and Nigel to finally meet Tamara and Bella for one last time prior to being kicked and beaten to death. Having finally satiated themselves with their varied humiliating punishments, George and Donald had dressed the two battered bodies in two of the oldest dresses (untraceable) from Donald's collection along with two pairs of the oldest high heeled shoes. To substantiate the case of the two being attacked while wearing female attire, Tim and Nigel – dressed in their new finery and appropriately made up – were subjected to a further kicking and beating. One hiccup had been trying to force a pair of stilettos onto Tim's extra-large feet. The ever practical Donald had resolved the problem by simply amputating Tim's toes using a pair of garden secateurs.

This gruesome little tidbit was never reported.

Early on the Monday morning, an hour before sunrise, the bodies had been driven to Clapham Common and left in a previously selected spot where they would lie undiscovered for a day or two. By ten o'clock George was in a meeting with Mr. Collick and the other directors at Sharp, Sharp and Collick and Donald, back at *Flori-Abundance*, was discussing the floral arrangements for a charity event being held that evening.

EYE CATCHING

Daniel surreptitiously eyed the well-known producer/director across the crowded room. 'It's fucking now or never,' he muttered to himself. 'C'mon, Danny boy, it's *your* turn to enter the lion's den!'

'Mr. Volare,' – a statement not a question – said Daniel having crossed the room and now facing the man. Deliberately ignoring the querulous looks of the man's companions he added, 'Daniel Markham. I'd like a word!'

Valerio Volare, a tall, gaunt figure, his lustrous hair drawn back into a long, thick pony tail, his pale, skull-like face a replica of Edvard Munch's sinister *The Scream*, looked at the insolent young man, an expression of disdain forming on his ghostly features.

'I *beg* your pardon?' said the producer/director in a hushed, deeply accented spectral tone. 'Does Valerio Volare *know* you?'

'No,' said Daniel boldly but thinking, Seeing I'm now well and truly inside the fucking lion's den I'd better deal with lion! 'But you will!' he said confidently, his voice unwavering.

'I will?' said VV (as he was known), a sinister smile beginning to play on his thin, bloodless lips. 'And pray, Mr. er... Mayhem, why would I be doing that?'

Daniel being the same height at the tall Italian returned the sarcastic jibe with a direct stare, his eyes flickering momentarily in confusion due to the distinct cast in VV's eye.

Focusing on the man's left eye Daniel, taking a quick breath, said even more boldly, 'Because I am the person destined to play Profirio Rubirosa in your next planned film!'

'Oh really? How interesting and you are err... your name again?' questioned VV with a yellow, wolverine smile.

'Daniel, Daniel Markham but my stage name is Daniel Defoe,' said Daniel.

'So Mr. *Defoe*,' smirked VV, running his eyes approvingly over the tall young man, taking in his handsome chiseled features, dark wavy hair, piercing green eyes and athletic frame, 'what is it exactly that you've *got* that makes you the err... as you say "person destined to play Rubirosa" in my next production?'

'Because,' said Daniel emboldened by the man's interest, however slight, 'I've read all about him, studied him intensely. I know all about his loves and err... his superior endowment.'

'Most enterprising of you Mr. Defoe and you seriously believe you can live up to the legend of the man, mentally and especially physically? You are obviously aware my films are famous for their nudity and graphic sex scenes. Profirio Rubirosa was once described by a some fortunate female as having a penis the size of a large pepper grinder, fourteen inches to be exact.' VV gave a snigger, 'Are you about to tell me Mr. Defoe...'

'I'm more that *up* to it, Mr. Volare,' said Daniel, playing heavily on the innuendo.

'Seeing is believing,' came the soft reply. Ignoring his stony-faced companions VV added without hesitation, 'The Pharaoh Suite, eleven o'clock.' With a final crooked glance at Daniel (Yes, you *do* have a severe squint Mr. V, thought Daniel) the producer/director turned back to his disgruntled companions.

'Eleven o'clock precisely,' said VV on opening the ornate door leading into the luxurious suite. 'Come in, Mr. Defoe. Come on in.'

Daniel, following the tall thin figure through to the sitting room of the suite was amused to see VV already wearing a dressing gown, a pair of Gucci slippers on his feet. Audition time, Danny boy, he mused. Well, Mr.

Volare, the proof of the penis is in the viewing and they all say the proof is certainly there with mine.

'Sit down, sit down Mr. Defoe.' VV gestured to one of a pair of sofas, 'and please help yourself to a glass of wine. I don't serve champagne as I never drink it.' The tall man sat himself down elegantly on the sofa opposite Daniel – as requested – pouring himself a glass.

'So,' said producer/director gazing across at Daniel, his squint even more apparent. 'I don't believe in foreplay so as soon as you've had a few sips of your wine – by the way the wine is from my own vineyards, delicious don't you think? – I want you to stand, strip, get yourself hard and then move over to where I am sitting.'

Fucking hell, thought Daniel, Talk about getting right down to it! Instead of sipping Daniel simply drained his wine with a noisy gulp. Placing the glass on the low coffee table between them he stood up. Taking off his jacket he unbuttoned his shirt and unbuckled his belt. Removing his shirt he dropped his pants. He wasn't wearing any underwear.

'Very impressive, Mr. Defoe,' said VV, his skull-like face expressionless. 'And you're not circumcised which is also good. My *Rubirosa* – like myself – is not going to be circumcised whether he was or not. That's one piece of information I have not been able to find out.' Here VV allowed himself a slight snigger. 'Now, get yourself hard and move across and stand right next to me.'

Daniel, his impressive cock growing steadily in his gently pumping hand, did as requested.

'Good, very good,' said VV, his thin feral tongue sliding out and momentarily wetting his lips. 'Now I want you to begin masturbating yourself slowly right next to my right cheek and when you are about to come you must do *exactly as I tell you*!'

I'm coming!' groaned Daniel, his engorged cock about to burst.

With a deft movement VV popped out his glass eye. 'Into the socket, into my eye socket!' he gasped. 'Push your cock's head into my socket as you come!'

A stunned Daniel, completely missing the target also missed getting the part.

ABOUT THE AUTHOR

Robin Anderson, an internationally known author and interior designer was born in Scotland and brought up in the former Southern Rhodesia (now Zimbabwe) and South Africa. Before attending Rhodes University (the Oxford of South Africa) he hosted his own radio programme in Rhodesia ('The Golden Voice of Teenage Half Hour!) and worked as a cub reporter on 'The Bulawayo Chronicle' during his gap year.

Leaving South Africa, he spent the early Sixties working with interior design companies in Paris, New York and London. He set up his own design company in London in 1970. Although interior design had been his first interest, the designer never stopped writing. Nowadays he makes numerous television appearances and is a regular guest on selected radio programmes, gives regular lectures on his writing.

His first novel, REGINA, A NOVEL OF SOME EXTREMES, was published in 1998. The novel gives a salacious look 'behind the scenes' of the glamorous but bitchy and competitive world of interior design, following the path of the unpleasant but talented Reginald Forbes as he cuts a swathe through the lives of his many unsuspecting victims.

Though London-based, the author travels extensively and the benefits of this are apparent in the various settings to his books. The Amazon, the Yucatan, Borneo, Myanmar, China, Russia, Japan, Sri Lanka, India, Egypt, Morocco, Kenya, Australia, The Maldives, Mauritius, Central Europe, Canada, North and South America plus the majority of the Caribbean Islands have also been visited. He has walked the Inca Trail in Peru; climbed Mount Kinabulu (Borneo) and Mount Kilimanjaro (Tanzania).

The author is a strong believer in the protection of endangered species. In 1959 he took part in 'Operation Noah' which involved the rescue of hundreds of animals from the rising waters of the new Kariba Dam being across the mighty Zambezi River in the north/western part of Zimbabwe.

He is also the proud 'foster parent' to four Orang-utans living at the famous Orang-utan Sanctuary in Sepilok, Borneo plus two elephants, Marlene and Marlon, who live happily on a ranch in Zimbabwe.

In a total contrast to the above, he also helped with the salvaging of precious works of art and manuscripts in Florence, Italy, during the Sixties when the River Arno burst its banks and flooded a major part of the ancient city.

In between his travels Anderson lives mainly in a spacious studio 'overlooking a glorious, leafy square' in London's exclusive Chelsea and a small hideaway in the Cinque Terre in his beloved Italy.

'Have laptop, will write and will travel!' is his mantra. In addition to these collections of short stories, *Thirteen Tales of Textual Arousal Volume One* and *Volume Two* the author has – to date – published a further sixteen novels with 'more on the way!'

ROBIN ANDERSON 2012
www.robin-anderson.com

a novel by
ROBIN ANDERSON

BRUISED
FRUIT

DEFUNCT GRISTLE

a novel by

ROBIN ANDERSON

Paul Dot Go

Robin Anderson

Nazca
Plains

A NOVEL BY
ROBIN ANDERSON

STILL
LIFE

A
BONER
BOOK

ANDERSON

STILL LIFE

THIRTEEN TALES OF TEXTUAL AROUSAL

a selection of tales by

ROBIN ANDERSON